The Truth About Melanie

John David Harris M.Ed.

Matador
Unit E2 Airfield Business Park,
Harrison Road, Market Harborough,
Leicestershire. LE16 7UL
Tel: 0116 2792299
Email: books@troubador.co.uk
Web: www.troubador.co.uk/matador
Twitter: @matadorbooks

ISBN: 978 1803137 193

British Library Cataloguing in Publication Data.
A catalogue record for this book is available from the British Library.

Printed and bound by CPI Group (UK) Ltd, Croydon, CR0 4YY
Typeset in 11pt Georgia by Troubador Publishing Ltd, Leicester, UK

Matador is an imprint of Troubador Publishing Ltd

This book is dedicated to my five lovely daughters.

Acknowledgements

To Nicholas Peters, First Officer, flying the Airbus A320.

My grateful thanks for all your help in ensuring aircraft procedures referred to in this book bear a resemblance to reality. Any mistakes remaining are my own.

Chapter 1

COMPARED WITH THE frequently drizzle-soaked English countryside, the mild and inviting climate of the Mediterranean often appears as an extremely attractive alternative, but in the past, it must have seemed light years away. However, with the advent of cheap commercial flights, tens of thousands of people suddenly became able, and only too glad, to exchange their fifty weeks of leaden grey cloud for an assured fortnight of sunshine and skies that sparkle with a perpetual blue – conditions that had the power to soothe the frantic mental pace engendered by life further north.

Many people in the great cities like London and Manchester would readily agree there is scant time to even glance up from the treadmill of life to appreciate the endless dreary canopy under which they labour. In fact, nightshift workers, such as hospital staff, are often continually exposed to the negative effects of artificial light or the even more questionable glare emanating from their computer screens. What about the essential health benefits of Vitamin D? Well, that's something that's just conveniently forgotten. And the air they breathe? Perhaps that would be better not asked.

The more years that pass, the greater the momentum seems to become, and it's an education to watch the rush hour in some of the cities' main underground stations – places where the sun never penetrates, and where the gods of hurry and agitation reign supreme. One has to wonder whether those locked into the tides of surging humanity are even aware of how subjugated their individuality has actually become; subjugated, in fact, to the heels of the man just in front or, better still, caught up in a struggle to outflank him at the slightest opportunity. It's almost fascinating to watch the fast-flowing rivers of people as they jostle and run around each other in a frantic attempt to reach their preordained escalator in time. But for what? The promise of an extra five minutes spent at home away from the endless demands of their office workplace. Moreover, this rodent-like existence is not confined to one occasion, but rules their lives five, even six, days a week; an endless repetition from which any attempt to escape would mean reneging on their mortgage and eventual homelessness on the polluted, uninviting streets. They know only too well there's no escape from the eternal carousel. However, such rigid lifestyles do not control everyone, as evidenced by a certain young lady and her companion as they approached Gate 12 at Gatwick Airport.

Surprisingly, despite her success, the girl in question – Melanie Jordan – known simply as Melanie – had never excelled at school. In fact, she had frequently been the despair of her teachers, who had often felt that with a little more effort she could have done so much better. But her interest had always lain elsewhere. She longed for the freedom that seemed to forever lie so tantalisingly just beyond the school gates. However, as she was to quickly discover, her longing was delusory, for once the protective shackles of education were gone, life lost no time in closing in with its incessant demands and time schedules so necessary for one's existence.

Restrictive incarceration never sits well with anyone, especially not for a girl of Melanie's disposition, who, right from early childhood, had so enthusiastically embraced the open liberty of the local recreation ground and the adventures it offered with various swings and roundabouts. That was not to mention the seemingly inexhaustible supply of trees and bushes that seemed to have been put there just to be explored. Even in the midst of all this self-expression, there had always loomed the vexed limitations of time. There had never seemed enough, and she would bitterly resent being told by her mother when they were due to go home for tea. I mean, who wanted tea anyway, when there was so much fun to be had?

'Oh, Mummy. Just a little bit longer,' she would plead.

Melanie was an only child, which tended, perhaps, to make her mother a little more tolerant than she might otherwise have been. This was especially true if her little daughter was happily playing with other children. In fact, during the summer months, the situation was often only resolved when the park keeper would apologise but insist it was time to lock the gates.

Knowing her child's character, Melanie's mother had hesitated to send her to any form of preschool, which, of course, was only a temporary stay of execution. The day of reckoning finally loomed with the approach of the little girl's fifth birthday, when there was no option but to broach the vexed subject of education and all that it entailed.

'Darling. In a few weeks,' she had said gently, 'you will be starting school. And that's very exciting, because you'll be meeting lots and lots of other children. And on top of that, you'll learn to read and write just like Daddy and Mummy.'

Her mother had tried on numerous occasions for another child to be a companion for her little daughter, but her efforts had always been without success. She'd fervently hoped that the thought of meeting other young pupils might help make the trauma of the first day just that little bit less daunting.

Melanie's parents had spent their entire married life in a small but comfortable terraced house in Shoreham, just off the main A27 westbound bypass. Situated on the south coast in the county of West Sussex, it was a modest sized but pleasant and busy

4

town located by the mouth of the River Adur. Its historic roots stretched back almost to the dawn of time, certainly to the Neolithic Age. Early settlers on the shores of England would have been only too glad to discover such an estuary where the town would one day stand.

However, there was more to the Adur than its estuary, for the river wound up through a strikingly beautiful valley and far inland towards its source in the Sussex Weald. Majestic hills rose sharply either side of the downland cleft, although how many millions of years it had taken for the river to carve its way through the dense chalk was an open question. Whatever time had been involved, the result was spectacular. The waterway had meandered back and forth across the valley floor to form lush green fields on either side of its banks; a haven that seethed with wildlife and farm animals.

Springtime in the Adur had always been a delight for Melanie, who loved nothing more than to skip along the riverbank among the myriad of brightly coloured weeds and buttercups, where she would spend hours in the sunshine selecting a bunch for her parents. Oh, for the joy of nature; freedom without limit; freedom to just do what made one happy. But then a shadow had begun to loom on her horizon: the shadow of school. And it was this time bomb that her mother was so desperately trying to defuse.

'Will I have to go every day?' Melanie asked anxiously.

In her mind's eye, her mother caught a glimpse of a caged wild bird as it futilely beat its wings against the unyielding metal bars in a frantic attempt to escape. It was only a fleeting mental image but spoke volumes concerning the human condition and its self-imposed constraints.

'No, darling, of course you won't have to go every day,' she assured her. Then, mindful of the birdcage image, she added, 'You'll still be free at weekends. And, in any case, you'll be home halfway through the afternoon.'

Her young daughter's crestfallen expression and look of apprehension had gone straight to her heart – although, as with other forms of childhood difficulties, such as illness, there was only so much a mother could do.

Christened June Somerville in 1955, Melanie's mother had led a quiet and uneventful life. In fact, she'd been born in the very house she now shared with her husband, Brian. After leaving comprehensive school at sixteen, she had worked happily at the local mushroom farm and thoroughly enjoyed the environment that had allowed her to see the wonders of nature first-hand. Moreover, like her small daughter, she also relished the outlying local countryside with its beautiful river and sweeping hillside views. June had always been fascinated by the change of seasons and was thrilled to see their rich and varied effects on the rural landscape. She found it a joy when, on rare occasions, the river had frozen over in the depths of winter and when its

6

banks had merged with the surrounding fields under deep rolling mounds of snow.

However, perhaps above all, she loved the early summer with its promise of the long and sun-filled days to come, when nature would burst forth into an abundance of colours in appreciation of the new year. Nothing gave June more pleasure than to stroll along the riverbank where she would gaze at the tall graceful white blossoms – or "milkmaids", as they were affectionately nicknamed. These would grow in abundance at the water's edge and mirror the river's course as it meandered far away into the distance. Sadly, those carefree days had passed all too quickly and now she had her own small child – although, in the strictest sense, Melanie was not hers. In reality, the little girl had been adopted at birth; something, rightly or wrongly, June had never divulged to anyone – not even the child herself.

Although not genetically related, Melanie and her mother shared many similar traits, but there was one very distinct difference between them. Whereas June would never consider herself unattractive, Melanie had always been quite striking from an early age. Thick honey-blonde hair framed a symmetrical heart-shaped face, while her large, vivid blue eyes stared out at the world with a beauty that was tangible.

Finally, however, the day approached for Melanie to be introduced to an existence of "not allowed to" – an existence governed by the sound of buzzers and bells, where people told you what to do and when to do it. School life had closed in.

Fortunately, situated not far from where they lived was a small Catholic primary school. While not particularly religious herself, Melanie's mother knew it enjoyed a favourable reputation and had therefore arranged an interview with the headteacher. However, not having seen a nun in full habit before had proved a somewhat daunting experience for poor Melanie.

Nevertheless, despite the strange regalia of the black hood and long flowing dark tunic, the headteacher turned out to be a kind and sympathetic individual with an obvious love for children, and Melanie had soon taken to her. Unfortunately, this in no way lessened the psychological impact of the following Monday – Monday 8th September 1986 – a day forever etched into her memory.

Once back home, Melanie had sat on the tiny swing in the garden behind their terraced house. It was not a big garden by most standards, but it had long been her world and contained many precious playthings from her earliest years. Perhaps the most prominent of which was the large playhouse that her father had constructed and where she'd spent many happy hours. There was the little slide that, somehow, had always just seemed to be there. How many times she'd climbed the small ladder to slip gleefully down its shiny metal surface would be too many to recall and the diminutive inflatable paddling pool had provided innumerable hours of fun during the summer months. As Melanie sat idly on the swing and gazed at these happy reminders, she'd been struck by a thought: a thought that reflected a maturity way beyond her years. *My truly free days are now over, forever.*

Now, as she edged her way towards Gate 12 at the airport, Melanie let her mind drift back over the intervening years and how she'd reached her current enviable situation. School had not been a great experience for her, although, ironically, her very last day had the most impact on her future and it came in the form of the rather timorous and aging careers teacher, Mr Jones. She'd always got the impression the man was afraid of his own shadow, so how he'd ended up amid the stresses and demands of a modern-day comprehensive school had always eluded her.

Anyway, just as she'd been clearing out her desk, with a hint of nostalgia, Mr Jones had wandered into the classroom. The rooms were interconnected, and he'd obviously only been on his way through, but, catching sight of her, he hesitated. Originally from the deep valleys of Wales and certainly in his late fifties, he stood little more than five feet two. The few grey hairs he'd got left curled forlornly about his ears. However, beneath this less than impressive exterior lurked an astute brain. Leaning his arms on the edge of her raised desktop, he observed, quietly, 'I understand this is your last day with us, but I suppose you're not really sorry, because I rather gather that school life has not exactly been your favourite thing.'

Melanie felt herself warm to his appreciation of her feelings.

'Oh, I wouldn't quite go as far as that,' she replied, while gazing round the soon-to-be-forgotten room. 'Although, I must admit I can think of better ways to spend my life.'

'Have you given any thought as to what you might like to do in the way of employment?' he ventured, tentatively. 'Because I don't believe you tried for any GCSEs.'

'No,' Melanie replied, with a certain feeling. 'And that's because I don't think I'd have stood a cat in hell's chance of passing any.' The diminutive Welshman had again smiled and nodded at her honesty. 'And as regards a job!' she exclaimed, satisfied now that her desk was quite clear. 'I'll probably get something at Johnson's mushroom farm where my mum used to work before she got married.' Then, closing her desk for the final time, she had added, 'The money's just about okay. It's also nice working conditions. And,' she emphasised pointedly, 'they don't need any GCSEs.'

The careers teacher again looked sympathetic. 'I think, Melanie,' he suggested, slowly, 'that although you may have no GCSEs, you might have overlooked one attribute you do have.'

'Oh?'

After asking her to wait a minute, the careers teacher had disappeared into the corridor and emerged a few moments later with a female colleague.

'I didn't like to mention the subject,' he continued, 'without another teacher being present. You have to be so careful these days. But it's my belief that you'd stand a very good chance in the world of modelling.' He looked slightly uncomfortable and shifted from one foot to the other as if finding it difficult to say what he had in mind. 'You must be aware,' he managed, finally, 'that you are a tall and very elegant young lady, and, I might add, with the looks to match.' He'd glanced at his colleague, who nodded in agreement; a teacher, Melanie remembered, from the lower school section, which catered for the twelve and thirteen-year-olds. As Mr Jones turned slowly and began to move away, he added, 'Well, it's a thought. At the very least, you could give it a try.' And with that, he and his colleague made their way out.

Mr Jones' observations were, of course, not news. Melanie knew, only too well, from the attention she had constantly received from some of the senior boys, that she was an attractive girl – although she'd seriously doubted whether this amounted to a modelling career. Moreover, the thought of such a glamorous life was a far cry from the humble working-class background of her parents. Therefore, initially, she'd not taken the careers teacher's suggestion very seriously and, as she'd said at the time, just planned to follow in her mother's footsteps working at the local mushroom farm.

About a year later, she happened to hear several other employees mention a summer beauty competition that was to be held near Black Rock, just off the beach in Brighton, and Mr Jones' advice suddenly sprang to mind. At that point, she had just turned seventeen and became determined to give it a try. However, she had much to find out, not least of which were her parents' reservations and the cattiness endemic to the world of modelling. Melanie's father, Brian, had been particularly vociferous in his objections over her entry into 'that kind of world', as he'd called it.

'I know, I know!' he had exclaimed from behind the relative safety of his newspaper and while lounging comfortably in his favourite armchair. 'The body beautiful and all that. And,' he stressed, 'I know artists have depicted it from time immemorial, but the fact remains that men are men, and in situations where there're a lot of attractive females openly displaying their femininity, then there's only one thing...'

'Dad!' exclaimed his wife. 'Don't be such an old reactionary.'

'There's nothing reactionary about the basic instinct of sex,' he had retaliated. 'I ought to know. I'm a man.'

'Well, that's what you've always assured me,' she grinned back. 'And I hope I've no reason to start doubting it now.'

'Anyway,' Melanie's father remarked, while folding his paper. 'I'll say no more. But that's my feeling about the situation.' Then, with an uncharacteristic directness, he looked straight at his daughter. 'What you finally decide to do is, of course, entirely up to you.'

Finally, and with her father's "blessing" still ringing in her ears, the day of the contest arrived. The actual event took place on the surrounds of Black Rock swimming pool, which was located towards the eastern end of Brighton's promenade. The weather that August Saturday had been nothing short of glorious. The pool was outdoors, and the water shimmered invitingly in the hot crystal-clear air. Even the perpetually grey English Channel had come up with some semblance of blue. Despite her resolve, when it had come to it, Melanie remembered feeling very nervous. The groups of glamorous young competitors idly standing about gossiping did little to help. Inordinately high heels and tiny bikinis had been the order of the day, and some of the egos present had seemed to be only surpassed by their owner's outsized hairpieces.

Melanie had chosen a two-piece red costume with high and elegant slim-fitting shoes to match. Beach huts had been provided for changing, but when stepping out to join the other competitors, she remembered feeling desperately conspicuous and isolated. This had probably been due to the fact that the other girls had chosen to wear their hair up, whereas she had brushed hers to a high sheen and allowed it to swing way down past her shoulders. Unfortunately, "shoulders" was the operative word, for she found most of them turned away in a distinctly chilly fashion. This was, perhaps, not altogether surprising, because it quickly became apparent that most of the girls present were semi-professionals who regularly competed on the beauty circuit. Melanie was a complete newcomer. Therefore, it was almost a relief when they were summoned by one of the judges to receive their number card and began parading round the pool; or, as her father had cynically put it, 'to begin the festival of the flesh'.

However, the event had been well supported by local people, who were crowded along the promenade railings and who showed genuine appreciation with rounds of applause. Melanie's mother had carefully watched the judges' expressions as they thoughtfully considered and gesticulated with their pencils. Finally, the parade had been called to a halt with the girls assuming practised poses, which involved an impressive alignment of feminine legs, as they awaited the judges' decision.

The actual results of the top three were announced in reverse order. Melanie had nursed a vague hope that she might at least have come in third place, but when that failed to materialise, she'd begun to lose interest. However, as the leading judge announced the winner for 1998, Melanie was stunned to discover that she had been picked as the new Miss Brighton. It would have been worth the trip to Black Rock just to see the sick expressions on the faces of her rivals as they realised they'd been trounced by a complete outsider. There was not a single "Congratulations!" nor "Well done!" Just an almost tangible air of resentment.

After the announcement, one of the judges came across to take Melanie's hand and lead her to the winner's podium. The runners-up were placed on either side and then he used a microphone to present her as the new titleholder. The announcement was followed by cheering from the audience and her mum shouting, 'Well done, Melanie. Well done!'

The final act had been for the outgoing beauty queen to drape the sash of honour around Melanie's shoulders. Although she struggled to place the coronet on her thick blonde hair, nevertheless, it had been a euphoric moment and one Melanie would never forget.

At this point in her reminiscing, Melanie had passed through check-in and security, and was on the final jet bridge that led into the aircraft itself. Putting her hand luggage down for a moment, she turned to her companion.

'I don't think I can ever remember it taking so long to get on board. What on earth are they doing up front?' she added, with a touch of irritation.

'Well, it's the height of the season and I imagine every seat is booked,' sympathised her friend. 'So, the cabin crew have probably got more than their hands full. It's not a job I'd fancy.'

Melanie took a moment to unobtrusively study her companion. Like herself, she was a tall, elegant young lady in her early twenties. Ironically, they'd met at the Black Rock beauty contest where she'd been runner-up and the only other competitor to offer her sincere congratulations. It had been a genuine warmth in a catty world and the two girls had been friends ever since. Their chance meeting had only been the second of three events on that memorable day that so impacted the following years, for as Melanie finally stepped down from the winner's podium, a smartly dressed young man had come forward and handed her a business card. Initially, she had suspected a come-on, but quickly realised the man was a professional and he represented a golden opportunity.

'Congratulations on your success,' he had smiled, with an irresistible charm. 'I must admit, I entirely agree with the judges; but more to the point, I'm a talent scout for the London agency, Top Models.' It had been a discussion he was obviously not going to protract, but upon turning to leave he had added, 'Anyway, if you happen to be interested, do give them a ring. I really believe you have a bright future.'

Melanie had made to reply, but he'd already moved away. *A chance meeting in the churning sea of life*, she thought. At first, she made no immediate move in response to the invitation. Instead, she discussed it with her parents in case there were any possible dubious implications that might be involved. Brighton's reputation alone for vulnerable young women was known to be something less than desirable, while London... Needless to say, her father had been dead against the idea.

'You just don't know what you'd be letting yourself in for,' had been his immediate reaction. 'The whole thing could be a front for a den of iniquity and God knows what else.'

Melanie knew her father meant well and was only expressing what he genuinely believed to be in her best interests. However, she was also aware that he belonged to the old ways of thinking, having held down a steady job in a local bakery all his life with little or no ambition. He was quite content to just keep the bills paid and live out his days in the same modest terraced house. Cautious reliability would have been a suitable epitaph. Although Melanie's mother was of a similar ilk, she had a little more fire in her veins, and it had been her encouragement that had finally persuaded Melanie to approach the London firm. The venture had not been undertaken alone, for Christine – the girl she had met at Black Rock – also decided to go along, not only in the hope of a modelling career herself, but to lend a little moral support as well.

Melanie had grown accustomed to the lingering looks of admiration she received from passing men, but as she and her friend had initially settled into their seats on the train to Victoria Station, two other passengers, laden with luggage, had joined them in the four-seater compartment. Overweight and obviously under-washed, they looked a thoroughly undesirable pair, and their entry had resulted in a tight squeeze with the two girls crouching up as close to the far side of the compartment as possible.

After exchanging covert looks of disgust, they had concentrated on the scenery as it flashed past the train window, with Melanie instinctively tucking her shapely legs back against the carriage seat. Neither of the girls had even dared glance at the unwholesome pair and had been only too glad when the men had finally disembarked at Haywards Heath.

'Phew!' exclaimed Christine after their departure. 'I'm glad to see the back of those two. I could almost feel that fat one undressing me with his eyes. And the stink...!'

Melanie eased herself away from the window. 'I'm just glad we live in an age of open-plan carriages,' she sighed. 'Can you imagine what it would have been like in the old days when trains consisted of individual compartments? If those two had got in, we'd have been trapped.'

Her friend looked thoughtful. 'That's true. Although there was always an emergency cord and if there was any trouble, you could pull it to stop the train. But of course,' she added, 'that would have depended on whether you could reach it.'

Melanie hated the lunacy that was Victoria Station and the insane buzz they had encountered on their arrival did little to change her opinion. Losing no time, the two girls made a beeline for the Underground and thence to their final destination, Top Models, eventually discovering the imposing-looking building just off Oxford Street. But at this point, feeling slightly overawed, Melanie had hesitated and it required all of her friend's encouragement to get her to operate the entry-phone system. Finally, they passed into an impressive foyer. Even then, it had fallen to Christine to approach the receptionist and explain the details of their appointment, where, upon seeing the business card originally given to Melanie, the highly manicured young woman rose from her seat with a curt, 'This way, please.'

How the receptionist maintained her balance in such incredibly high heels was a complete enigma to Melanie, for they made anything she'd ever worn look like flatties. However, with a practised wiggling of the hips, the young woman had obviously mastered the required technique.

Like the beauty competition, that London trip had proved a turning point for both girls and was one that had set them on the road to success and a standard of living they could only have dreamt about. For Melanie, there was a second and quite different reason that had made her visit to the city so memorable. The agency booked them into a four-star hotel that night while contracts were being drawn up for signing the following day. Anticipating this eventuality, Melanie had brought a light travelling bag that contained a few basic necessities. As she had lain back on the luxurious bed surveying her sumptuous surroundings, she was struck by a sudden thought – and it was not the first time the anomaly had occurred to her. Swinging her elegant legs off the bed, she got up and reached for her bag before pulling back the zip.

On the rare occasions when away from home, Melanie had always packed a double-sided wallet that contained photographs of her parents. That evening, she reverently lifted it from its resting place to gaze at the two monochrome images.

Encased in oval-shaped surrounds, they depicted a couple in their mid-twenties. Although not beautiful, her mother had been a pretty girl with a warm expression and short dark hair that framed an oval-shaped face. Neither of her parents were particularly tall, with her father standing barely five feet eight and her mother perhaps an inch or so shorter. Brian, with his rugged features and curved, rather oversized nose, could hardly be described as handsome – although he had been blessed with a head of dense, heavy black hair. Cautious by nature, he rarely laughed. But that was not to say he was without a rather acid sense of humour, which he could apply to great effect. Somehow, though, it all made Melanie wonder.

Laying the still-open wallet on the bed, she crossed the room and viewed herself in front of a full-length mirror. Normally she would have used the facility to make a final check on her appearance before venturing into the great unforgiving "out there". That evening, she studied herself for an entirely different reason. Having discarded her dressing gown, she carefully examined her reflection from head to foot and saw a tall, lithe young woman, of almost perfect proportions, standing something approaching six feet.

This critical appraisal had nothing to do with any sense of conceit, as she observed her beautifully accentuated cheekbones and the almost perfect symmetry of her facial structure; qualities which, when combined with her large blue eyes and heavy blonde hair, made for an extremely sensual impact. Yet, grateful as she was for this outpouring of nature's benevolence, it nevertheless left her wondering – wondering how she could be so physically different from her parents. True, she shared her mother's joy of nature and her restrained no-nonsense attitude to life, but as regards the rest... She glanced at her parents' photographs. Was it even possible that she could have been the result of a far-off genetic throwback to some Saxon ancestor? Or was there another, less palatable, explanation of which she had no knowledge? Before finally drifting off to sleep, she determined to raise the matter with her parents once and for all – although, in the event, her career in the world of fashion advanced at such a pace that the opportunity was destined to not arise for some time.

Melanie quickly switched her thoughts back to the present as they finally set foot on the aeroplane and found themselves face-to-face with the smartly uniformed and very handsome captain, who, upon seeing the two beautiful young women, immediately dispensed with the traditional 'Welcome on board' mantra normally reserved for Joe Public. Seeing his hesitation, Christine was quick off the mark.

'Hello, Captain,' she smiled. 'I know you'll take good care of us.'

Dimples appeared at the edges of the chief pilot's mouth. 'You can depend on it, ladies. You can absolutely depend on it.'

After they'd taken their seats, Christine turned to her friend. 'That man fancied you,' she grinned. 'But then again, come to think of it, what man doesn't?'

'Oh, rubbish!' exclaimed Melanie, modestly. 'It was you who made the impression.'

Finally, with their hand luggage safely stowed away in the overhead storage locker, Christine covertly indicated that the captain was just about to enter the cockpit.

'That's a very attractive man and yet you showed absolutely no interest,' she observed. 'In fact, when I come to think of it, you've never shown a great deal of interest in any man.' But then she suddenly looked contrite. 'Sorry, it's none of my business anyway.'

'No, no. That's fine,' Melanie hastened to assure her friend. 'It's not that I'm disinterested, but, as you know, in this game it seems you're never in one place long enough to form any relationships.' She paused uncertainly for a moment, and then admitted, 'Although, if I'm honest, I suppose I am a bit choosy and cautious when it comes to men.' And looking earnest, she added, 'I would need someone who would love me and care about me for my own sake and less about... Well, you know what.'

Christine did know what. Only too well. Standing up, she suddenly started rummaging in the overhead locker. Finally snapping it shut, she returned to her seat and handed Melanie a book.

'Holiday present,' she smiled. 'I bought it on our way through the departure lounge. I got one for myself as well. I thought a little light reading might help us relax.'

In view of subsequent events, it's questionable whether the expression "light reading" had been appropriate, because she could have had little inkling of just how far-reaching the effects of her gift would ultimately be. However, as Melanie glanced at the book's cover, the plane's jet engines suddenly assumed a deep-throated roar.

'This,' Melanie exclaimed apprehensively, 'is the bit I really don't like. I'm always afraid there won't be enough runway before the plane takes off. It has happened, you know,' she stressed, unleashing her fear on her friend, but then sighed in relief when feeling herself being tilted back as the aircraft lifted its nose and soared up towards the blue. Leaning over to the window, she could see the pattern of England's green and pleasant land dropping away, finally becoming obscured by masses of gently drifting grey clouds. 'Off at last,' she breathed, glancing down at the title of the shiny new paperback: *Straw Hat*. 'That's a strange title,' she mused, flicking through the pages. 'What made you choose this book in particular?'

'Oh,' replied Christine, casually, 'I just heard somewhere that the author's quite good. In fact, my own book is by the same writer.'

The two friends settled down to enjoy the flight and the beginning of a four-week well-deserved holiday after nearly three unbroken years in the pressured world of fashion and the catwalk. Their destination was Menorca – one of the Balearic Islands – and a place that basked for many months of the year in southern sunshine. Situated at the western end of the Mediterranean, the island group owed its origins to titanic upheavals of volcanic activity in the mists of antiquity. It was only necessary to look at the various strata of rock that had been systematically laid down by successive outpourings of lava to appreciate the full fury the earth must have unleashed during the agony of the island's birth. Then, the whole area would have been a very inhospitable place – a place of infernal heat with rolling banks of dense black smoke interspersed by sheets of flame that shot hundreds of feet up into the impenetrable sulphur-ridden atmosphere; a place, in fact, where no living organism could have survived. It seemed impossible to imagine that the now tranquil location that attracted hundreds of thousands of visitors each year could conceivably owe its origins to such utter chaos.

Christine lolled back in her seat with its view of the plane's huge-looking metallic wing, which glinted in the sunshine and stretched out over the blue. Impressive as it appeared, it nevertheless seemed hardly adequate to support the full weight of the massive jet engine suspended under its structure and she glanced sideways at Melanie.

'It makes you wonder, you know,' she observed idly, 'how the wings can carry the engines... I mean, they seem so big and the wings don't look all that sturdy to me.'

'Oh, don't!' protested her companion. 'I feel nervous enough already with all those miles of nothingness between us and the ground.'

'Is everything alright?' came a sudden, unexpected voice. Turning towards the aisle, Melanie found herself facing a very smart and courteous flight attendant. 'It's just that I couldn't help overhearing your concerns,' continued the young woman. 'I'd like to assure you that all of this company's aircraft have to undergo regular and exhaustive testing.' She smiled and paused before offering them both a drink from the trolley she'd been carefully steering down the aisle. But scarcely were the words out of her mouth than the aircraft lurched and seemed to drop frighteningly. Melanie thought her last hour had come and looked ghastly. The unperturbed hostess just smiled again. 'Turbulence. Nothing to worry about; it's quite common.' Then, after handing them each a capped cup of hot coffee, she continued on her way.

'Phew!' gasped the blonde model, collapsing back against the headrest and nearly spilling her hot drink in the process. 'I know I'll love Menorca, but I hate the business of getting there.'

However, even as she spoke, her friend leant across and pointed excitedly through the porthole. 'Look. It's the island.'

And sure enough, far below, she could see the sun-kissed landscape with its numerous white-walled buildings and red tiled roofs. However, from such a height, everything looked so unbelievably tiny, and as the plane banked in preparation for its final approach, it became possible to see great swathes of their destination.

'It's a bit how God must see everything,' mused Christine.

As Melanie turned to her new book, it seemed only moments later that the airline's jingles sounded followed by details of their arrival at Mahon Airport. The multiple clicking of seatbelts further reinforced the fact of their imminent landing – although, landings and their imminence were the final horror for Melanie, and she turned tentatively to her friend.

'Now this is the bit that I also really, really hate,' she confessed fearfully. 'I always think they bring the plane in fast and try to stop too quickly. I'm terrified that it will end up with its nose in the runway.'

Not devoid of fear herself, Christine appreciated how Melanie felt and took her hand. She winced as the undercarriage wheels hit the ground so forcibly that the aircraft bounced slightly before again coming into contact with the tarmac and finally shuddering to a halt.

'Rough. Very rough,' muttered Christine. 'But at least we're down safely, so let's get out and start enjoying ourselves.'

Of course, it's never quite that easy. All the other passengers had the same idea and were already on their feet, scrambling and scratching at the overhead lockers. Nobody seemed willing to give way to anyone else and, initially, the two friends found themselves confined to their seats. In fact, by the time they finally managed to retrieve their hand luggage, they were among the last to leave the aircraft.

However, the delay was not without its compensations. Their exit lay towards the nose of the aircraft and close to the space normally reserved for the cabin crew during any off-duty moments. It was also where they had first met the captain and, as they prepared to leave, he suddenly emerged from the cockpit area. Although there was no way she could be sure, Christine suspected it was more than just coincidence. Coincidence or not, though, she had to admit he cut a stunning figure. Standing some six feet three with his peaked white cap bearing the airline insignia and wearing the tailored company uniform, he was, indeed, a man she could have gone for in a big way. Unfortunately, as she had realised initially, his interests lay elsewhere – namely, with her companion, who by this time was outside the exit.

The captain apologised for the earlier air disturbances. 'I just hope it wasn't too frightening,' he insisted. 'But even though we do our best, it's something us pilots can't always avoid.' He'd obviously been talking to her, but his eyes constantly strayed towards Melanie and, finally, he ventured to call out, 'I'm sorry, but I'm afraid I didn't catch your name.'

By this stage, Melanie was beginning to show signs of impatience – a fact demonstrated by the agitated swinging of the holdall hanging from her shoulder. Finally, however, she responded by looking slowly at the speaker. She was tempted to say that the reason he didn't catch her name was because she'd never intended giving it. On the surface, the whole thing was beginning to look like a classic overture, yet Melanie sensed that perhaps there was more to the captain than angular good looks and a well-honed body. With his low-pitched foreign-sounding voice and kind blue eyes, Melanie was beginning to think that, at last, perhaps she might be looking at a man she'd always subconsciously sought. The possibility prevented her from shouting out an initial reaction of 'Come on, Christine. Let's get the hell out of here.' Instead, she was surprised to hear herself reply softly, 'Melanie. My name's Melanie and the lady you're talking to is my friend, Christine, and we're here on a well-deserved break in Cala Blanca.' The few remaining stragglers were, by now, well on their way to the main airport terminal, which left the unlikely trio with the flight deck to themselves. As she spoke, the dimples round the chief officer's mouth deepened in a broad smile.

'Well,' he responded in the same low-key voice, 'If I may introduce myself, I'm Captain Jörgensen. Karl von Jörgensen, to be exact. But I always think just Karl sounds more friendly.'

German! she thought suddenly. Knowing her grandparents had been terribly wounded during the Second World War blitz, she'd always been very cautious of anything east of the Rhine.

However, her new acquaintance quickly sensed her hesitancy and nodded.

'Yes, German, I'm afraid,' he admitted. 'Worse, my grandfather was also a pilot. But in his case, he used to fly the Junkers 88 bombers.' He took a step forward and pleaded that he had nothing to do with that generation, but then paused as if unsure to voice what he had in mind. Finally, he suggested, 'I'm due off in a few days myself this week and I'll also be staying in the Cala Blanca area near Ciutadella. And,' he emphasised, 'I intend to spend most of my time in the sea.' He smiled, before adding, hesitantly, 'So... possibly we might bump into each other again.'

While all this was going on, Christine felt as though she might just as well have dropped through the floor out of sight.

'You know,' continued the captain. 'It's rare that I have the opportunity of flying two such beautiful ladies as yourselves. And,' he added with a slight bow, 'it's been a great pleasure.' Then, turning to re-enter the cockpit, he added, 'I do hope you both have a lovely holiday. It's a beautiful island and the swimming here really is an absolute joy.' Then, with a click of the intervening door, their unexpected exchange was over.

'Well,' breathed Christine. 'He really was something else.'

'Yes, wasn't he just!' exclaimed her friend. But then, snapping back to the realities of the moment, Melanie added, 'Come on. Let's get to the luggage reclaim before someone pinches all our stuff.'

Christine had grown to know her companion very well over the time they'd been together. She was well aware of her friend's sense of independence and love of freedom, which, she suspected, had made her hesitant about forming any deep relationships. Although Melanie would be the first to deny it, there had been many opportunities. But this time...

Standing by the conveyor belt waiting to snatch their bags, Christine covertly glanced across at her friend's expression. She'd been right; the pilot had made a big impression.

Chapter 2

THEY'D RENTED AN expensive villa that afforded sweeping views across the Mediterranean. It was an unquestionably breathtaking location, but it lay far to the western side of the island and entailed a long drive on the right-hand side of the road – or, depending on one's point of view, the "wrong side".

Melanie had arranged for the use of a car during their holiday with a well-known hire company and the vehicle should have been waiting for them on the airport forecourt. However, although the area was literally teeming with cars belonging to other firms, there was no sign of their own transport, and after a journey that had entailed trudging wheelie suitcases along seemingly endless miles of airport corridors, it felt like the last straw.

They waited in vain and scanned the area for any sign of their car. New to the welcome heat of the island, their goal had been to get to their destination as quickly as possible and dive straight into the pool behind the villa, not to frustratingly sweat it out for hours on the airport forecourt. Melanie was the first to collapse wearily down onto her suitcase.

'Wonderful,' she muttered dispiritedly. 'Just wonderful. Why the hell can't they get it right? You pay the money, you make certain they have all the flight details, and they still can't—'

But just as she was getting into a fully fired-up moan, Christine interrupted, 'If it's a Blue Line car we're expecting, I think it's just pulled into the car park opposite.' Sure enough, after much bowing and scraping, interspersed with what sounded like apologies in Spanish, the keys were finally handed over. Then, with their luggage safely stowed in the boot and Melanie behind the wheel, Christine leant over to whisper a tactful word of warning. 'Don't forget they drive on the right over here. So, remember to give way to vehicles coming from the left – especially at roundabouts.'

'I know, I know!' exclaimed Melanie, a touch impatiently. 'I have driven abroad before, you know.'

Christine did know, and knew only too well, from their early days together when camping just outside Lyon in France. It had been barely daybreak as they had pulled out of the campsite – a manoeuvre that had involved an initial sharp left turn. However, instead of crossing over to the right-hand lane, her friend had a mental blip and nearly taken them under the front wheels of an oncoming articulated lorry.

In some respects, the friends were quite dissimilar. Christine tended to be quiet and perhaps a little introverted, while at the same time thinking things out carefully. Melanie, on the other hand, was far more spontaneous and outgoing.

The hour's drive from Mahon Airport left both girls feeling tired but overjoyed as they finally pulled up outside their white-walled villa where the stunning views from the car momentarily held them spellbound. It was early August, around 7pm, and, as they gazed out over the sea, the absolute tranquil blue of the Mediterranean defied description with its serenity being further enhanced by a pathway of gold as the sun slowly sank towards the western horizon.

'Beautiful. Just beautiful,' breathed Christine. 'And yet,' she sighed. 'Think of all those people in the big cities either complete prisoners in their cars or slaves to the endless rush-hour rat race on the underground.'

'Oh, come on,' interrupted Melanie, brightly, 'we haven't come all this way to philosophise on the human condition. We,' she insisted, 'have come to have some fun and that's just what I intend to do. Now, let's get our luggage inside and these hot bodies in that pool.'

So, their first day ended with two huge displacements of water as, finally and thankfully, the girls hurled themselves into its cooling depths.

Early the following morning saw Melanie relaxing on the villa balcony with the sun slowly gladdening the eastern sky as she enjoyed a freshly brewed coffee. At the same time, she imbibed the freshness of the air that is usually only found during the first hours of the day. The balcony was fronted by a low classical balustrade and overlooked extensive areas of rugged volcanic rock, where differing colourful cacti and other wild vegetation had gained a toehold in virtually every available crevice. Sitting there in the early morning light while savouring her coffee, Melanie couldn't help thinking she'd be quite content to spend the rest of the day just soaking up the peace and watching the white-sailed yachts as they glided silently by. Equally attractive was the occasional huge white seagull that would chance its luck and land on the balcony rail in the hope of any crumbs that might have fallen from the small coffee table.

However, all this relaxed mental drifting was suddenly interrupted as Christine emerged from the villa, clad in a brief, if not provocative, two-piece costume and obviously bursting with ideas for the day.

'The bay of Cala Santandria!' she exclaimed enthusiastically, while slapping a guidebook on the table. 'It's virtually just around the corner and it's got a huge sandy bay; perfect for sunbathing. And there're two great restaurants—'

'Have you by any chance,' interrupted Melanie, 'had your early morning swim? If not, it might help tone down some of that energy.' But seeing Christine's expression, she quickly relented. 'Good idea. Let's get our things and give it a try. We could also have breakfast while we're there.'

It was, of course, the height of the holiday season and as the two friends approached the beach, they found themselves besieged by a sea of brightly coloured sun brollies. The problem was, they all had occupants who were busily devouring every last inch of shade they could get their skin under. It was still early in the morning, so it made them wonder what it would be like later in the day.

Melanie was the first to plonk her bag and towels on the sand in frustration, and even that was on what little there was still available. Many of the couples lying indolently about on the warm ground were initially either too lazy or too engaged in various stages of endearment to notice the girls were even there. But Melanie and her friend were far from two ordinary girls. Frequenters of the world of high fashion and glamour, they looked every inch the part, and whether various female partners liked it or not, male heads with bodies of various qualities and degrees of tan were beginning to turn in their direction.

'I think,' began Christine, 'we should have allowed a bit more material for our costumes. They may be okay at the villa pool, but I'm not sure about the impact they're having around here.'

Melanie was just about to describe her total disregard for whatever the local male population might think, when her attention became diverted by a Spanish-sounding voice.

'Ah! *Señoritas*. You very much need a sun brolly, no?'

Turning to trace the speaker, Melanie found herself gazing down at a swarthy, rather diminutive Spaniard, who, by his expression, seemed only too pleased to help. But this, she suspected, arose from the euros he would charge rather than any concern for their welfare.

'*Sí*,' she replied, mimicking the Spaniard's tone. 'The *señoritas* very much need a brolly. Yes.'

'Gosh, this sand is hot,' protested Christine, as they followed their miniscule, but welcome, saviour.

'It's all a question of a cheap pair of flip-flops!' exclaimed Melanie. 'I did mention it before we came.'

Finally, their benefactor indicated a rather jaded-looking pair of sunshades leaning forlornly up against a pile of volcanic rocks. Situated as they were at the back of the beach and not far from the refuse bins, Christine was not surprised they'd been left to their fate.

'*Sí*, you like, *señoritas*?' But with no alternative, the girls just exchanged glances while enquiring how much.

'Twenty-five euros for the day!' exclaimed Melanie after the shady little Spaniard had departed with their money. 'Bloody robbery. And he didn't even offer to put them up for us. Pig!'

'Never mind,' responded her more conciliatory-minded friend. 'At least we've now got our own spot of sand and some shade. So, I suggest you leave your sunhat and our valuables with me while you go and enjoy a swim. It looks absolutely fantastic out there.'

Christine was right. Warmed by the earlier months of sunshine, the sea was a perfect temperature and crystal clear, with a sandy floor that slowly shelved away into deep water. Once up to her waist, Melanie finally surrendered to its silky embrace and struck out towards the mouth of the bay. Most of the other bathers tended to stick to the shallows, but Melanie's goal was to find a part of the sea that she'd have more or less to herself and the sense of quiet that went with it.

Finally reaching an area virtually devoid of people, she lay back on the water and allowed herself to float while gazing up at the clear blue sky overhead. The noise from children playing in the shallows had grown faint and the only disturbance – if you could call it such – came from a circling seagull as it swooped low to enquire who dared venture into what was, after all, its virtual sole preserve.

The bay was formed by a vast gap in the rock and, like the island itself, represented the vestigial remains of an unimaginable upheaval eons ago; an age when the lava would have run and bubbled like boiling water. Fascinated, Melanie turned over and swam towards one of the towering cliffs where she gently explored parts of its rugged surface just above the waterline. Wherever she looked, the rocks were riddled with small round holes that had once been the domain of scalding steam. Now, however, it seemed as though the titanic upheaval had suddenly frozen in time as if to bear witness to the monumental events that had once taken place there so long ago.

At this point, Melanie was probably treading some forty feet of water so clear that it allowed for a view right to the seabed – a view that included shoals of fish varying in both size and colour as they darted about in seemingly preordained directions and groupings. It was a coordination that baffled Melanie as she watched how hundreds of the creatures would suddenly change direction as if by some undetectable directive. But then, her idle speculation instantly evaporated as she felt a sharp pain just below her knee, which was closely followed by a second one on her ankle. Glancing down, she shuddered involuntarily at the sight of several semi-translucent entities with long trailing tendrils drifting around her legs, and one was hovering in a particularly sensitive location. Even though they were the less noxious type of jellyfish, they could still impart a nasty sting and Melanie lost no time in powering away from the area. Why God should ever have designed such foul things completely eluded her and she was only too glad to re-join the pandemonium going on near the beach.

As Melanie thankfully set foot back on the dry, warm sand, she noticed Christine busily waving to get her attention. Finally plonking herself down beside her friend, she was presented with the most indecently sized cornet she'd ever clapped eyes on. The ice cream alone must have been at least nine inches high and was in the form of a multicoloured spiral.

'I do suppose, you know,' protested Melanie, 'that, as professional models, we need to keep an eye on our waistlines.'

'Oh, get it down you,' protested her friend, while taking the first bite. 'We're on holiday, remember.'

'How could I forget?' retorted Melanie, indicating

the angry-looking punctures on her legs. 'I certainly didn't get those in the English Channel.'

'How on earth...?'

'Jellies!' exclaimed Melanie, adjusting her sunhat and snapping on her dark glasses. 'Believe you me, if you go for a swim, it's probably better to rough it in the shallows with the kids and their parents.'

'I'll bear that in mind,' replied Christine as she got to her feet. 'Oh, and by the way, keep a look out for that fat bloke over there by the restaurant. If ever I saw a lech, it's him. I'm just sorry for his poor wife, because he's been eyeing me up and down the whole time you were in the water.'

'It's known as "pleasure by looking",' smiled Melanie. She raised her sunglasses and gazed in the direction Christine had indicated. 'Oh, I see what you mean! It's that guy at the corner table. I don't know how the hell he manages to keep that overhang he calls a stomach clear of the ground. Anyway, I doubt whether he would pose much of a threat.'

Having finished the vulgar-sized ice cream, Melanie settled down on the blanket and luxuriously stretched out her endlessly long legs. Copious amounts of protecting sun cream had been applied, but she was nevertheless still careful to limit the time her skin was exposed to the sun, being forever mindful of the damage it could cause. However, once comfortably settled, she turned to her friend for a favour.

'Christine,' she pleaded, 'before you go, would you be an angel and get me a coffee?'

Her statuesque friend spun round with her hands on both hips in a playful stance of defiance.

'Are you asking me to skirt all the way around that fat guy just to get you a coffee?'

'Er, yes. Something like that,' smiled Melanie. Then, finally, with the requisite drink in her hand, she waved Christine off as she entered the shallows. 'Mind the jellies!' she called out.

Christine responded by pointing her forefinger towards the restaurant. 'Mind the lech!' she mouthed

By now it was approaching 11am and, turning on her side, Melanie reached for the spare towel before rolling it into a cushion to support her head. Total relaxation in an idyllic location. She breathed a sigh of contentment while finishing off the coffee and then, with nothing else to do except soak up the beauty of the bay, she unzipped the side pocket of their beach bag and removed the book her friend had so thoughtfully bought for the trip. *Straw Hat*. She again pondered on its title. In hindsight, she would often wonder whether the strange sequence of events that eventually unfolded owed their origins to the Brighton beauty competition or to events here in the picturesque bay of Menorca.

Melanie was a quick reader and rapidly became absorbed in the plot. As she moved on to the second chapter, something out in the water caught her attention; a thin line of foam was heading straight for the beach. Obviously the backwash of a strong swimmer, she continued to watch with a certain fascination as the man reached the shallows and finally stood up. Ripping the snorkelling gear from his head, the unknown swimmer strode purposefully through the remaining water to finally stand on the sandy foreshore. At first, she thought he was the airline pilot – Captain Karl von Jörgensen – for he and the man she was looking at shared a similar, almost perfect, physique. However, Melanie realised this individual was slightly taller with wider shoulders and well-defined muscles that spoke of hours of dedicated gym work.

As Christine had observed on several occasions, Melanie had always been cautious when it came to men and, although the pilot had made a big impression, when Melanie looked at this man she felt the earth move. However, as the stranger started up the beach, she quickly reverted her attention to the book, having no desire to be caught staring – although, she found it all but impossible to concentrate and covertly watched the swimmer's progress as he moved in the direction of the car park. But then, to her horror, as the object of her attention drew level, he suddenly paused and turned in her direction. Finally, standing barely a few feet away and with the snorkel gear still dripping in his left hand, he observed casually, 'Good book?'

If ever she'd had to play it cool, this was the occasion and, although almost trembling with emotional reaction, Melanie took her time to answer. Slowly and deliberately, she removed her dark glasses and studied the stranger. Her normal response would have been along the lines of, 'Yes thanks, if it's any of your business.' But this was something different – very, very different – for here was a man among men; a stranger who needed no fashionable stubble to emphasise his jawline and with an almost perfect physique that still glistened with droplets of water after having powered through the sea.

Seeing her hesitancy, he apologised. 'Oh, I'm sorry. I do assure you this is not a come-on. It's just that the story you're reading was my idea... And, well, sometimes it's nice to know if people enjoy it.'

'You mean,' she finally managed, albeit slightly incoherently and while glancing down at the paperback's cover, 'that you're...?'

He smiled slightly before turning away, but then added, almost as an afterthought, 'Oh, by the way, I should warn you that everything has a very sad ending.' Then, after a further pause, he casually mentioned that people sometimes referred to him as John Grant.

But it didn't make sense, and again looking at the book's cover, she protested, 'I thought your name was John Harris.'

However, Christine had chosen that very moment to race up the beach for a slice of the action, but as Melanie turned back to her visitor, he seemed to have vanished without trace. Puzzled, she carefully looked round the bay, but try as she might, could see absolutely no sign of the enigmatic stranger. It was almost as though he'd dematerialised into thin air and a frightening thought flashed through her mind. Had she just dreamt the whole thing? But the thought was almost immediately dispelled by her friend's reaction.

'Wow!' she exclaimed. 'Where did he spring from?'

'More to the point,' retorted Melanie. 'Where has he sprung to? I just turned around and he was gone.'

'Oh, he was probably just on the pull anyway.'

'Men like that don't have to go on the pull, as you put it,' protested Melanie. 'I tell you, he was the finest example of the male gender I've ever seen.'

'Well, I wouldn't argue with that,' smiled her friend. 'And he's obviously got through to you.'

After further scanning the area, Melanie finally gave up and sat down beside her companion.

'It's very, very strange,' she exclaimed, while ignoring Christine's remark. 'One moment he was standing here talking to me, and the next he just seemed to vanish.'

'But,' enquired Christine, persistently, while turning to lay on her side, 'what made him speak to you in the first place?'

'Well, believe it or not, some men actually find me attractive,' grinned her fellow model. Then added, 'No. I'm only kidding. The fact is, he claimed to be the author of the book you gave me.'

'Now, you've got to admit that's a different line,' rejoined Christine with fresh interest, as she raised herself up on her elbows.

Melanie shook her head. 'I don't believe it was just a different line. I really think he was the genuine article.' She reached to scoop up a handful of the warm dry sand and let it dribble slowly away in a fine stream. Then, finding that, even with dark glasses, the sun at that time of day was so fierce it made her frown, she immediately turned away from its direct glare.

'Well, I can tell you I wouldn't mind a bit of his direct attention,' grinned Christine.

Ignoring the remark, Melanie murmured, 'It was odd because he said something quite strange. Well, at least, I thought it sounded strange.'

'Oh?'

'Well, what he actually said was, "Oh, by the way, I should warn you that everything has a very sad ending."'

'There's nothing peculiar about that!' exclaimed Christine. 'Lots of books have sad endings. And if he really was the author, then surely, he should know.'

But they were words that were to prove all too prophetic.

Melanie shook her head again, while slowly gathering up another handful of sand. 'The point is, I'm not quite sure how he meant it. In some ways, it could have been that he was referring to the events of real life. Oh, I don't know,' she added, throwing the sand to one side. 'Perhaps it was just my imagination – in fact, I'm beginning to wonder if the whole episode wasn't my imagination.'

'He looked solid enough to me,' affirmed her companion. 'Almost too solid! But, you know, it's an interesting point, because, when it comes to it, I've

44

always wondered how we can really be sure what is imagination and what is reality.'

At this, Melanie adjusted her sunglasses for the umpteenth time and shook her blonde locks loosely about her shoulders, before reaching for a brush and proceeding to groom them virtually strand by strand. Finally, she observed, 'When you really come to think about it, I suppose you never know.' Melanie had never been one for deep thought and was struggling with her friend's observation. 'I mean, I saw him, and I heard him, although I didn't actually touch him.'

'Shame!'

'Well, shame or not,' Melanie retorted, 'two of my senses told me he was there and, at the end of the day, all we've got are our physical senses to know what is real. But,' she speculated slowly, 'if we end up losing our minds, then I suppose it's possible to start experiencing almost anything – even to a point where you could live a reality that doesn't exist. I remember once, as a child, I had a high fever with measles and used to see all sorts of horrible things crawling over my bed. But, of course, they weren't real because my imagination was out of control.'

'Are you quite sure,' Christine smiled, 'that you're not talking about real events a bit later in life?'

Her reward for that particular gem was a playful whack from the hairbrush.

'Another thing that I found odd,' Melanie frowned, 'was the way he referred to himself as John Grant. That's the fictional name of the chief character in the book you gave me.'

Her friend shrugged. 'Perhaps that's his real name and he writes under a *nom de plume*. Or... perhaps in some weird way he likes to identify with one of his imaginary characters.' But Christine's thoughts were suddenly interrupted.

'Hello there.' She heard a vaguely familiar voice – a greeting accompanied by the most blatant flannel. 'The two most beautiful ladies on the beach, if I may say so.'

For the briefest moment, Melanie hoped the stranger had returned, but then she recognised the slightly guttural tones of Captain Karl von Jörgensen, the airline pilot – although, she had to admit, he was formidable competition; with a deep tan and a towel draped round his shoulders, he exuded an air of absolute health and vitality.

Suspecting where his real interests lay, Christine turned on her side and randomly thumbed through the pages of her book in an apparent display of indifference. However, events were to turn out rather differently to how she might have expected.

By this point, the sun had reached its zenith and the hot atmosphere, together with the clear blue sky, made the cool-looking water of the bay seem an ever more attractive proposition.

'I wondered,' ventured the bronzed pilot, 'if I could tempt either one or both of you ladies to come with me for a swim.' He accompanied the invitation with one of his dimpled smiles.

Had it not been for her recent encounter, Melanie would have almost certainly jumped at the offer. However...

'Well,' she began tactfully, 'I've only just been in and, I might add, got stung in the process. But I'm sure Christine would be pleased to go with you. Wouldn't you, Christine?' she emphasised with a covert nudge at her friend.

Christine would and did – albeit with a feigned air of reluctance.

Although less forthcoming than Melanie, Christine was, by any standard, a beautiful and statuesque young woman. Dense auburn hair flowed freely over her shoulders to reach her waist; a feature kept partly in check by a wide-brimmed sunhat. The overall effect was quite dazzling. As she rose to remove her hat and coil her locks under the protection of a swimming cap, the pilot could scarcely believe his luck. Finally, side by side, they reached the edge of the water.

'If I get stung,' she observed, with an uncharacteristic playfulness, 'I shall blame you.'

Having reached ankle-depth, Karl raised his right hand in a mock oath. 'I do hereby promise to undertake full responsibility for any bites, stings or other forms of marine molestation that might come your way,' he smiled.

'I'll hold you to that,' she asserted, as the water rose to their waists. He responded by pointing across the bay to a small restaurant that was perched high on the volcanic cliff and which afforded extensive views out to sea.

'How about sharing a glass of wine over there?' he suggested. 'If you feel you can swim that distance.'

A remark for which he was rewarded by being drenched with copious handfuls of water.

'It's a lovely idea,' she agreed. 'But how do you actually reach the place?'

'Well, if you look carefully, there's a metal ladder that runs up from the water to the restaurant. So, what are we waiting for?' He grinned as he powered forwards towards their objective. However, the restaurant was farther away than it appeared, and by the time they finally congregated at the foot of the ladder, Christine was quite exhausted and only too glad to clutch at the rungs while catching her breath.

'Sorry,' apologised Karl. 'Perhaps we should have taken it a bit more slowly.'

Finally, and still dripping wet, they arrived at a table that, complete with its colourful parasol and extensive views, made an idyllic spot. Shade was also provided by a number of well-spaced and graceful palms, while the bar, which had been uniquely carved into the living rock, added to the overall charm of the location.

'Beautiful. Absolutely beautiful,' breathed Christine as she unfastened her bathing cap and released her abundant hair to its own devices. 'I hate wearing that,' she muttered with obvious relief. 'But I have to protect my hair, especially in our work. But it makes me feel so ugly – quite apart from the fact no one else ever wears one.'

The pilot leant forwards with both arms on the table. 'With or without it, you're an extremely glamorous young woman. And I'm proud to be in your company.'

'And that includes my friend?' she retorted, almost abruptly.

Karl just grinned his dimpled smile.

From their position at the edge of the restaurant, they could look straight down at the water where shoals of fish were busily darting about scooping up any odd scraps of food thrown by various patrons. When Christine looked back at the beach, the people there appeared almost like ants – although she could just about make out her friend and she waved vigorously. However, Melanie was deeply engrossed in her book and appeared not to notice.

Melanie had noticed and finally acknowledged her friend's greeting, although, deep down, she felt she'd missed out – especially after watching them both swimming away so happily together, almost, as it were, towards a new and exciting life. The sight had left her feeling slightly isolated and alone.

Back at the cliff-side restaurant, a sharp exchange had begun between Karl and one of the waiters. It was all conducted in fluent Spanish, so Christine had no idea what it was about. However, from the attendant's expression and the way he shrugged his shoulders before turning away with his hands raised in despair, she got the distinct impression he was a far from happy man.

'Well, what caused all that?' she asked, while running her fingers through her hair. 'It didn't sound very pleasant.'

'Yes, sorry,' apologised the pilot, 'but his nibs,' and he covertly indicated the retreating waiter, 'took exception to us sitting here in swimwear. Clients,' he added, 'should dress more modestly while dining in his restaurant.'

'Oh, it's his place then? I thought he was just—'

'No,' asserted her new companion. 'He actually owns the place.'

'Well, perhaps we should...' And Christine made to get up. But Karl put a restraining hand on her forearm.

'It's okay,' he stressed. 'He's agreed to serve us this time, but in future he can bloody well stuff his restaurant.' She noticed that it had been said with a certain guttural edge, reminiscent of his Germanic origins, and Christine felt a pang of caution, mindful of how her grandparents had always referred to such men as people you didn't mess with.

Finally, as they were begrudgingly served with two elegantly slim glasses of Rioja, Christine raised the obvious question. 'Since my purse is back on the beach with Melanie, how do you propose paying for this extravaganza? Especially since the owner already seems about to explode at any minute.'

The dimpled smile flashed again. 'My secret,' he exclaimed, while tapping the top of his meagre trunks, 'is a tiny, waterproof money-belt. So, drink up and enjoy. And let us toast to a glorious and memorable day.'

However, the glorious and memorable day was passing all too quickly as the blinding sun slowly began to dip towards the horizon visible beyond the entrance to the bay.

'It's only an idea,' suggested Karl, 'but we could have a meal here.'

Draining the last of her wine, Christine smiled back across the rim of her glass. 'I'd love to if old rodent-face would go along with it – which I somehow doubt. What with us being in an advanced state of undress and all that.'

In response, Karl glanced across at the proprietor, who was busily engaged with enchanting more suitable clients.

'I see what you mean. With that spiky little moustache and pointed chin, he really does convey a certain rat-like quality. I might even mention the similarity to him when we next order.'

'Don't you dare!' she hissed back in alarm, but then smiled as she recognised his distorted sense of humour. 'In any case,' she exclaimed, 'I can't desert my friend any longer.'

'I understand,' he nodded, 'but I won't let you go without one last drink together.'

Finally, as they prepared to leave and Christine clipped the chinstrap of her bathing cap in place, her companion risked a question.

'You mentioned your work. Would it be rude of me to ask what you actually do?'

As the question was put in such a genteel way, Christine was happy to reply. 'Melanie and I work as fashion models – top of the range stuff. All our assignments come through an agency based in London.'

He would have loved to ask more, but somehow

felt that he'd already pushed his luck far enough. However, as they prepared to leave, he noticed she looked slightly apprehensive.

'It's that metal ladder,' she explained. 'It's so vertical and slippery.'

'Look,' he assured her, 'I'll go down first and steady you until we get into the water.' For a moment, he turned away to look across the bay and frowned at the dazzling radiance of the sinking sun. 'I was wondering, perhaps,' he began uncertainly, 'if I might have your mobile number before we part company?'

Now, Christine had not come on holiday looking for a partner or with any intentions of forming a relationship, although she would readily have admitted to being enthralled by the company of such an elegant and professional man. Nevertheless, she was still slightly hesitant over anything that might cause them to meet up again, but, slowly, her smile broke through.

'Why not? But how will you remember it if I tell you?'

For the first time, and with an expression full of admiration, he looked straight into her eyes.

'Believe you me, I'll remember it.' Then, before reaching the ladder, he turned and called out to the proprietor, '*Adiós amigo*. It was good to know you,' and he completed the gesture with a throwaway mock salute.

Rodent-face ignored him.

Finally, having reached the bottom of the ladder, and with the silky clear water lapping about their shoulders, the German expressed his gratitude for her company.

'A lovely day spent unexpectedly with a beautiful young lady.' He shook his head and smiled. 'It doesn't come any better than that.' Sadly, it was one of those magical moments that was gone almost before it had begun. 'I'll see you safely across the bay,' he volunteered. 'Then I must go.'

So, side by side, they swam leisurely back towards the beach where they'd left Melanie. Finally, with them standing waist-deep in the water, Christine unbuckled her bathing cap and uncharacteristically threw caution to the wind.

'Just for the record,' she ventured, whilst skimming the palms of her hands idly over the surface. 'Tell me, would you sooner have had my friend with you for that drink?'

For the briefest moment, everything fell deathly quiet – even the joyful cries and splashing of nearby children somehow ceased to exist. But her companion's response instantly broke the spell.

'If I'm honest, *ja*. Although, that was at first.' He gently placed his hands on top of her arms and smiled. 'Now, I wouldn't exchange our time together for anything or anybody.'

After that, he strode away through the shallows in the direction of the car park. However, his going left a slightly disconsolate Christine to softly murmur, 'Fly safely, my pilot. Fly safely.' Prophetic words that one day she would recall only too well. She watched him until he reached the water's edge, where he turned and waved before blowing her a kiss. And then, scarcely able to believe what she was doing, she immediately responded with a similar gesture. Eventually, with him completely out of sight, she waded through the remaining stretch of water to her friend, while all the time wondering if she would ever see or hear from him again.

Back on the beach, Melanie looked up with a mixture of surprise and curiosity.

'Well, I must say that all looked very cosy,' she observed, drawing her heels up through the sand. Then, laying down her book, she turned to one side and rested on her elbow. 'Hardly like you to go doe-eyed over someone you've barely met,' she added in her blunt and rather frank way. 'And don't deny it. I saw you blowing kisses to each other.' Melanie sat up abruptly. 'You do know, I suppose, he's German.'

'So...?' rejoined her friend, taking her seat on the sand. 'He's also a human being.'

'And a far too handsome one by the look of it, if your expression is anything to go by! Incidentally, have you made any arrangements to see him again?'

If Melanie had not been her close friend and virtually constant professional companion, Christine would have told her to keep her nose out. But, 'No,' she answered. 'Nothing concrete.' She sighed. 'He asked for my mobile details, but he's probably got a girl at every airport. So, I don't expect I'll hear from him again. In fact, I doubt whether he'll even remember my number.'

'It seems to me,' smiled her fellow model, 'that you might have avoided the jellyfish, but got stung by something a lot bigger instead.' Then, picking up her book, she observed more soberly, 'Strange how we've gone for years without really meeting anyone in particular, then two very special men turn up on the same day, but only to almost immediately vanish off into the blue.'

'In my case,' agreed Christine, while reaching for her beach bag, 'very much off into the blue, if you don't mind me saying so.'

A week later again saw the two friends on the beach at Santandria, but this time they'd learned their lesson and arrived early enough to grab a choice spot near the water's edge, which also came complete with a huge sun brolly. However, no sooner had their bottoms hit the ground than the euro-hawk descended.

'That'll be just thirty-five euros, please,' demanded the diminutive Spaniard.

'What?' shouted the enraged Melanie. 'I could buy one for that price.'

The tax collector shrugged indifferently. '*Sí, señorita.*' But then he added pointedly, while indicating the rising sun, 'I tink it will be a very hot day today, no? And with no sunshade!' He again shrugged, which left the two girls with little alternative but to hand over the extortionate amount.

'Blackmail,' muttered Melanie, darkly. 'Sheer bloody blackmail. If that stranger I met yesterday had been here, that snitch would have ended up face down in the middle of the bay.'

Christine unzipped her beach bag and began to roll out a towel on the sand. 'Just because this mythical hero of yours was built like a gladiator, it doesn't mean to say he would behave like one!' And with that, she stretched out to allow the warm balmy air coming off the sea to flow over her like the gentle caress of fine silk.

The beach had been comparatively deserted upon their arrival, but was now rapidly filling up with holidaymakers of various shapes and sizes – a quality shared by a lot of their offspring who, with their screaming and splashing, seemed hell-bent on reducing the shallows to a no-go area. Melanie pulled a face and rolled her eyes.

'Just try not to listen!' exclaimed Christine. 'Better still – finish that book I bought for you.'

The elegant blonde lay down beside her friend to share some of the gentle warm sea breeze. 'Actually,' Melanie replied, 'I finished that book last night; very unusual story and, in some ways, very sad.'

'Oh?' began her companion. But even as she spoke, two unsavoury-looking males decided to plant themselves on the narrow strip separating the two friends from the water's edge. Worse, their eyes seemed everywhere, and most notably in the direction of the two girls. Obviously Spanish and sporting tattoos that stretched from their waists to the top of their shaven heads, they constituted a very undesirable pair. Neither model could speak a word of Castilian, but from the tone of their voices and raucous laughter, the subject of their conversation was only too obvious. Finally, the scrawnier of the two got up and made his way over towards Melanie, but his approach heralded a rampant smell of garlic, while his scruffy jaws indicated only a passing relationship with a razor. Although barely five feet eight and of slender build, he still managed to sport a beer belly of which many men would have been proud. His whole image, in fact, made Melanie shudder. She thought briefly of her encounter with the stranger who had called himself John Grant and wondered how two such different men could belong to the same species.

However, it was a shock that didn't end there, for when the man spoke it was in fluent English as he indicated a tall building on the far side of the beach. '*Señorita*, may I have the honour of your company over a glass of wine at the hotel?'

Melanie knew what she would like to have said, but managed to restrain herself and declined with a blunt, 'No, thank you.'

At this rebuff, the Spaniard seemed to become angry and drew himself up to his five feet something and declared imperiously, 'Do you not know that I am Don de Borze? Elder son of the de Borze family.'

Now, Melanie's sense of freedom had always included self-expression – a habit that, on occasion, had got her into trouble – and she didn't hold back this time.

'Look. If you were the King of Spain, the answer's

still the same. Now do us both a favour and get the bloody hell out of my face.'

Then, still undeterred, the Spaniard made a serious mistake, which was probably due to not being fully sober after a night's carousing. But mistake it was, because instead of backing away graciously, he reached for the model's arm.

'Just one little drink will do no harm, no?'

Although, harm it did, for the incensed model immediately and furiously leapt to her feet and brought her right hand crashing across his face with such force that the slap could be heard halfway around the beach.

'Don't you dare touch me,' she almost screamed as the man staggered back.

The situation was getting quite ugly and other people in the area were beginning to take notice. Finally, a bronzed and muscular young holidaymaker stepped forward and, although a complete stranger, Melanie somehow sensed him to be a German. She was right.

'*Stört dich dieser mann?*' he asked the furious model, in guttural tones.

Although unable to speak the language, she was nevertheless quick to realise his concern. 'No, no,' she assured him. 'It's all over and we're just about to leave, but *danke schön*.' Then, struggling to express her gratitude further, she said slowly, 'It was very kind of you to come to our rescue,' and smiled to emphasise her thanks.

The German raised both hands and shook his

head. 'It was nothing,' he just about managed in broken English before turning away to re-join his friends.

'Come on, Christine!' exclaimed Melanie while gathering up their belongings. 'Let's try the beach at Cala Galdana. Perhaps we might get a little more peace over there.'

During their journey, Melanie was quiet for a while as she studied the road ahead.

'You know,' she observed, 'I've never learned the German language – and certainly not at that bore-house they called a school. But in a strange way, when I hear it spoken, it somehow sounds familiar. Almost as though...' She paused. 'Oh, I don't know. It's almost as though I've been German in a previous life. In fact, I sometimes feel I originated from that part of the world. Which is a nonsense, of course, because I was born and brought up in Shoreham, Sussex.'

'Well,' replied her friend, cautiously, 'from the way you handled that man back there, you certainly displayed a hint of the German race. You really hurt him, you know.' She shrugged. 'It's not my place to criticise, but he only asked you out for a drink.'

Melanie slumped guiltily at the wheel. 'Yes, I know,' she admitted, 'but I hate being mauled – especially by strange men. I tell you what, though. While I think of it, there's something I want to show you when we get back to the villa.'

The friends motored on for several miles in companionable silence as they both enjoyed views across the rocky and rather arid landscape so particular to the island. Finally, Christine observed, 'You were in the process of telling me how sad the ending of your book was. At least you were, until that "in-yer-face" Spaniard showed up.'

'Yes, well,' began Melanie, while pulling into the Cala Galdana car park. And then, leaning back in her seat, she added, 'I don't want to bore you with too much detail, but, briefly, it describes a middle-class family who acquired a beautiful painting that turned out to be some kind of time portal, through which a tragedy from the past almost destroys their lives. But,' she emphasised, turning to Christine, 'the bit that really got to me was the hopeless love between the man of the family and his little girl's nanny – a true love that could never happen because of his sense of duty and affection for his wife. He was much older than the nanny,' she continued, while managing to find a space for their car. 'But the saddest part of all was how they only got together on the very day he died. Although, you know,' she affirmed with a sudden zeal, 'he came across as a very special man.' Then, looking out through the windscreen and across the sparkling Mediterranean, she added, 'In other words, very much like that stranger who claimed to be the author.'

'You mean, the one who did the disappearing act,' exclaimed Christine.

Her friend nodded. 'Yes – and the one I intend to track down if I get the opportunity.'

'You know, we've worked together for over four years now,' observed Christine, 'and this is the first time I've ever seen you serious about anyone.'

'This is the first time I've ever found someone worth being interested in,' Melanie retorted, while preparing to get out of the car.

The bay of Cala Galdana was a quite different experience to the one they'd just left, with various volcanic rock formations soaring high up out of the sea and with myriads of fish congregated in the warm clear water that swirled around their bases – an ideal place, in fact, for anyone who enjoyed the rewards of scuba diving. Nearby was an inviting restaurant, which stood on a high promontory and afforded far-reaching views out to sea. There were fewer people about, so the whole area seemed an ideal location.

'Right,' pronounced Christine, 'I suggest lunch followed by a rest and then each of us taking turns at snorkelling.'

Once back at their villa later, Melanie lifted her case from the top of the wardrobe and carefully unzipped the top section. Then, gently removing the wallet containing the portraits of her parents, she handed it to Christine.

'You've never met my parents, have you?'

Christine sat on the edge of the bed and shook her head. 'No. I don't know why, but it's probably because we've always been otherwise engaged with assignments in London or elsewhere, while I believe your folks are down on the south coast.'

Melanie nodded. 'That wallet contains a photo of my mother and father.' She then looked quite serious. 'If you would, I'd like your opinion on something – something I've brooded over for years.'

'Oh?' replied Christine.

And at that point, Melanie dropped her bombshell. 'You see,' she began, 'I've sometimes wondered if they really are my parents.'

'Heavens!' exclaimed a shocked Christine. 'What on earth makes you think that?'

Her friend drew a deep breath before sitting next to her on the bed. 'Well, have a look at them and tell me. Can you really see any resemblance to me? And I mean, any resemblance at all?'

The auburn-haired model studied the two oval frames carefully for several minutes, then looked back at her friend and shook her head. 'To be honest,' she began. 'No, I can't. They just look like two ordinary, kind and nice people. But I can't see they look anything like you.' Then, laying the wallet down on her lap, she added, 'Though that doesn't necessarily mean they're not your parents – you could well be some throwback to an earlier generation.'

'A long way back,' muttered Melanie, restoring the wallet to her suitcase. 'I've even thought I might have come from Prussian stock. I remember reading somewhere how whole lines of tall blond Prussian soldiers were mown down by British machine guns during the First World War.'

At this, her friend pulled a look of horror and shuddered. 'How awful. It's too terrible to think about – all those young lives wasted. And for what? A few feet of land at best.'

'But just look at the length of my legs,' insisted Melanie. 'They never came from either of my parents.'

'Well,' smiled her friend. 'Just be grateful. I certainly wouldn't complain!' But she went on to mention the sensitive possibility they had both avoided. 'Do you think, perhaps, you might have been adopted and never told?'

'Oh, I don't know,' sighed Melanie, wearily, as she poured them both a drink. Then, passing a glass to her companion, she added, 'I've tried recalling my earliest memories – you know, as far back as it's possible. But I can only ever remember them as my parents.' She paused for a moment and ran her forefinger thoughtfully across the rim of her glass. 'They've been brilliant to me, yet somehow there's always been that something at the back of my mind I could never quite identify.'

Christine lounged back leisurely while clasping both hands round her knees. 'Does it really matter?' she murmured. 'After all, you say they were good parents and still are. I think, if I were you, I'd leave well alone – not least because if you go digging about and come up with something, then it's really not going to do any good to the two people who've only ever loved and cared for you.'

Melanie moved to top up their glasses. 'You're right, of course. But it's just not knowing – and human beings are, by their very nature, curious creatures.'

'The real problem is,' explained her friend, 'the only way you can ever really be sure is to ask them outright. But can you imagine the bundle of laughs that would be? Think of it: "Excuse me, but are you my real parents?" I don't think so.' Christine took a long sip of her wine before getting off the bed and stretching.

'No,' smiled Melanie. 'You're absolutely right. It wouldn't be very pleasant. But,' she stressed almost aggressively, 'I'm bloody well going to track down the author of that book you gave me.'

'Ah! The mysterious stranger on the shore,' smiled her companion. 'Well, in that, I wish you luck. That's presupposing he even exists!'

Chapter 3

THE HOLIDAY SLIPPED pleasantly away until, finally, duty called them back to the UK; four weeks seemed to have gone by as quickly as four hours.

Their next few assignments took place between Edinburgh and Paris. They involved a great deal of travel and, in some cases, long hours on the catwalk facing a constant barrage of clicking cameras. It paid well, and in many ways was a glamorous existence that most young women could only dream about, yet, somehow, after her encounter with the mysterious author, Melanie now found herself increasingly irritated by the hordes of over-busy and effeminate men who seemed to frequent the world of fashion. Taking her friend aside on one particularly hectic occasion, she gave vent to her feelings.

'No wonder we never manage to find any decent boyfriends. I mean, look at the place! It's crawling with men who've only got eyes for each other.'

'I should keep your voice down when you're saying things like that,' Christine advised her. 'We're living in a politically correct world now, you know.'

She shrugged and shook her head. 'Freedom of speech? Forget it!'

'Look. Next week,' observed Melanie, ignoring her friend's warning, 'we're down in London to sponsor some new wonder face cream. Silk, I think it's called. Anyway, it should be an undemanding week and give me the opportunity to try and trace the author of my book. Apparently,' she continued, 'it was published by a group called Purple Shine and I intend to pay them a visit. Sooo... I wondered if you'd like to come along with me.'

'I don't know why you even bother to ask,' retorted Christine, while using her index finger to push the lens of a camera that had penetrated just a bit too far into their personal space. 'Do you mind?' she exclaimed to the photographer. 'Please allow us some privacy. Anyway, as I was saying,' she continued, still glowering at the offending cameraman. 'We always seem to go everywhere together anyway.' It was very true, because, almost from the first day after the Brighton beauty contest, they'd remained virtually inseparable.

The following week, the two friends stood outside of an ultra-modern and imposing glass and aluminium structure. It was the latest building in architectural style, with a soaring apex that reached far up into the sky and spoke deafeningly of how the London skyline would look in the future.

'How our world is changing,' observed Christine as she gazed around at the remaining classic Victorian structures, which, in their turn, would inevitably succumb to the unstoppable rush of commerce. 'Every time I visit the city, it seems different,' she added. 'And traffic! The air is not fit to breathe.'

Monumentally huge aluminium letters stretched diagonally across the structure to spell out the title, "Purple Shine Publishers".

'This is the place,' announced Melanie, triumphantly. 'So, let's see what we can find out.'

The reception desk was vast and manned by a number of attendants.

'I understand Purple Shine published this,' Melanie stated bluntly, while unceremoniously placing her book on the counter in front of one of them.

Faced by two glamorous women, the poor male receptionist was briefly taken aback. Finally, he managed a weak, 'Well yes. If it's got our trademark, it would have been published by us.' Then, nervously putting on a pair of thin wire-framed spectacles, he took a closer look. 'Ahem. This is definitely one of ours, but it was first printed years ago and long before my time.'

Melanie felt her patience slipping away. 'Look. I need to contact the author, so would you please be kind enough to take me to the editor or put me in touch with whoever was in charge when it was originally printed.'

Obviously the nervous type, Melanie's directness did little to help as he began to perspire around the hairline. 'I'm sorry,' he just about managed, 'but the editor is a busy man and you can't go barging in without an appointment.'

Christine could see that her friend was going about it all the wrong way and, leaning on the counter, she flashed her big dark eyes at the poor man.

'Do you think,' she asked quietly, 'you could ask him nicely if he could spare us just a few minutes?'

And, with that, the attendant reached for the phone. When he finally replaced the receiver, he indicated the lift. 'You're in luck!' he exclaimed, in the same feeble voice. 'You want Mr Jackson. It's third floor and last door on the right.'

Finally, Melanie and Christine found themselves in the presence of the god himself: a deity who obviously appreciated the goddess-like appearance of his visitors and who, from behind his wide-topped desk, invited them to take a seat. Again displaying her book, Melanie reiterated her desire to contact the author. However, the editor shook his head. 'I'm afraid to do that you would need the services of a medium, because he died a number of years before I took office.'

'But he can't have died,' protested a shocked Melanie, 'because we both saw him back on the beach in Menorca only a few weeks ago.'

'Well,' exclaimed the editor, 'whoever it was, it certainly wasn't John Harris who wrote that book – of that, I can assure you.'

Melanie looked at her equally shaken friend and again wondered if her brief encounter had been a figment of her imagination. Looking nonplussed, she finally asked the editor if there was any way he could help them. He looked thoughtful for a moment.

'All I know,' he replied slowly, 'is what I've been told by those who had direct contact with him at the time.'

'And?'

'Apparently he was a tall, well-built man,' observed the editor, 'and not one to pick an argument with.' He paused, then added, almost as an afterthought, 'In his later years, I believe he was suffering from a form of Alzheimer's disease. But look. You need to speak to my predecessor. He's retired and in his early nineties now, but he knew the man you're after quite well.' He jotted a few lines on a notepad before ripping off the sheet and handing it to his visitors. 'There, that's all the details you'll need to contact him. He's called James Chronestead – a very knowledgeable man. And I'm sure he'll be able to help. Oh, and by the way, do call him first.'

'Implying,' muttered Christine under her breath, as they left his office, 'don't just go barging in like we've done here.'

James Chronestead lived on the outskirts of a small country village in a remote part of Mid Sussex. His actual home turned out to be a very old picturesque cottage constructed mainly from timber and plaster and probably dated back to the 1500s. Tiny square windows peered out nervously at the great external world from beneath the frowning overhang of a heavy thatched roof. Although the whole property was set in a small, low, white-fenced plot of land, the garden nevertheless abounded with the bright competing colours of lupins, wisteria, and tall, elegant gladioli, clad with numerous delicate bell-shaped blossoms.

'It's so quaint,' murmured Christine. 'I wouldn't mind living in something like this when I get older.'

'Hmm,' retorted Melanie. 'You might find it a bit cramped after the luxurious hotel rooms we've become used to.'

The doorbell was operated by pulling a thin metal rod and, after Melanie's first attempt, the small oak door swung back to reveal a quite tiny gentleman, who, in the context of his accommodation, looked just about right.

'Mr Chronestead? Mr James Chronestead?' ventured Melanie.

'Ah yes. Quite so,' smiled the householder, warmly. 'But please, just call me James. You must be Melanie and Christine. I've been looking forward to meeting you, so please do come in. But oh, be careful of the drop, because with these older places, the flooring is lower than the ground outside.'

Once they were inside, it allowed for a unique experience – almost like stepping back several hundred years. Opposite the front door stood an ornate flintstone fireplace flanked on either side by two high-backed armchairs. Both were covered with the same floral motif material that had been chosen for the curtains. The two small windows they graced admitted a limited, yet warm, light and seemed to endow everything with a certain gentle harmony.

Immediately to the right, and positioned beneath one of the windows, stood a small round dining table complete with four antique chairs, while the brilliance of its sparkling white tablecloth was almost blinding. Transfixed, Melanie's attention finally came to rest on the bookshelves, which were packed with every conceivable title and consumed the entire west wall.

'Ah!' exclaimed their host. 'Can I offer you ladies a cup of tea or anything?' And, indicating the table, he added, 'Please do take a seat.' He gave a slightly sad smile. 'I have so few visitors at my age, so I have to make the most of those who do come and see me.'

'Yes, thank you. Tea would be nice,' smiled Christine, 'and I know my friend would enjoy a cup.' Then, as their host disappeared to prepare their refreshments, she whispered, 'The loneliness of old age.'

'It comes to us all eventually,' replied Melanie. 'Well, that's if you live long enough,' she added, taking a seat by the window. With domestic sounds emanating from the small kitchenette, she thought out loud, 'I wonder if Mr Chronestead has been married and had a family.'

Finally, their host reappeared complete with a tray and a set of bone china tea cups containing steaming hot tea. Setting it carefully down on the table, he promised to return in a moment, and sure enough he was back almost immediately laden with a sugar bowl and milk jug.

'There,' he declared. 'All we need. I hate getting up for something immediately after I've just sat down.'

'It's a beautiful tea set,' admired Melanie, as she looked around the room. 'Everything matches in your lovely little home.'

'Well,' smiled their host, as he passed the biscuit barrel, 'if you can't be comfortable in your later years, you're never going to be. But changing the subject, when you were on the phone you mentioned a certain book and wondered if I might be able to help.'

At this, Melanie reached into her handbag and withdrew the volume entitled *Straw Hat*.

'Ah, yes!' exclaimed the old boy as he picked it up off the table. 'This was the last novel the author wrote.' He paused while flicking through its pages and shook his head, before adding, 'It was very sad, you know, because I witnessed his mind slowly deteriorate as it was being completed.' Then, laying the book down almost reverently, he observed, 'He'd always been such a strong man, both physically and intellectually, and to see him decline like I did was very... Well, I'm sure you must understand.'

At this point, Melanie stepped in. 'Mr Jackson, the current editor of Purple Shine Publishing, told me he'd died a number of years ago.'

'That's quite correct,' nodded their host, before offering them more tea and topping up Christine's cup. 'I was at his funeral.'

'But this is what I don't understand,' said Melanie.

72

'A few weeks ago, I was lying on a beach in Menorca reading that very book, when a man approached me and claimed to be the author.'

'Well, it couldn't have been the author—' James began.

But Melanie hastily interrupted him. 'He didn't hang about, but, as he left, he said some very strange things. One was that everything would end very sadly, and the other was that some people would know him better as John Grant. But,' she objected, 'that can't be right, because the real author's name is John Harris. Well, that's what it says on the cover, anyway – so I just don't know what to think.'

For a long time, the retired editor made no reply, but just sat absently stirring his tea. Finally, he spoke. 'How old would you say that man was?'

'Oh, certainly in his prime. Thirty-five to forty, I'd say. Well, somewhere thereabouts,' replied Melanie.

James nodded slowly. 'And can you describe what he looked like?'

At this invitation, Christine nudged her friend. 'Go for it, kid!'

Melanie responded with a disapproving glance. Then, tilting her head slightly, exclaimed, 'He was certainly in excess of six feet three and muscular. Oh, and,' she added, 'he was also very handsome with thick dark-brown hair, which tended to hang down across his forehead.'

James again nodded. 'That sounds very much like the man I knew. However,' he observed thoughtfully, 'you have to bear in mind that it might have been someone who claimed to be the author and just happened to resemble him. I suppose you don't remember the date and time of the encounter?'

Melanie thought for a moment. 'It was the first day after our arrival.' She turned to Christine for confirmation. 'He appeared while you were out swimming, remember? But the date,' she murmured, 'that would probably have been the 8th. Yes, that was it. Wednesday 8th July. And the time?' She shrugged. 'Late morning. Eleven-ish, maybe.'

On hearing this, their host glanced across the room towards his prolific array of books, and seeing their curiosity, he smiled. 'My collection of diaries. I started them when I was just nine and I've kept up the habit ever since.' Getting to his feet, he moved over to run his index finger along the orderly line of their spines. Finally, he withdrew the volume marked "1987". 'That was the year we lost John,' he murmured, and returning to their table proceeded to thumb through its pages.

'The 8th of July, as you rightly said, fell on a Monday this year,' he added, thinking aloud, 'but this is 2002 and I'm looking back some years to when it fell on a Wednesday. The point of all this,' he said, catching sight of their puzzled expressions, 'is that John died on July 4th, fifteen years ago. Now, his funeral took place on the 8th with the final stipulation that his cortege should stop briefly at the gates of Ley Farm.' He tapped the book that was still lying on the table, before adding, 'That was the backdrop for his novel.' Their host resumed his seat and, bearing down on his forearms, he peered at them over the edge of his open diary. 'What I find strange, or at least a strong coincidence,' he observed quietly, 'is that the funeral procession halted at 11am precisely.' And with that, he closed the diary. Then, leaning back in his chair, he slowly and deliberately repeated what he'd just said. 'At 11am *precisely*. Can you believe that? The very time you say you saw him – or, at least, someone like him – on the beach in Menorca.'

'Well, as you say, it's certainly a coincidence,' replied Melanie, while taking the liberty of topping up her cup from the teapot. 'But I wouldn't call it exactly earth-shattering. I mean, what are you trying to say? That, at 11am, the author jumped out of his box just to pay me a visit on some remote island in the Mediterranean?' Her expression was a picture. 'Come on now,' she added.

Christine looked askance at her friend's reaction and was quick to voice her feelings. 'Melanie. James has been very hospitable and he's only trying to help. There's no need to be offensive.'

The old man smiled. 'No offence taken. There are a number of factors of which you are unaware. You see,' he continued slowly, 'Ley Farm is a real place and not somewhere John just dreamt up. What's more, he visited there on a number of occasions while researching the story.' For a moment, their host stopped as if words seemed to fail him and, reaching across the table, he helped himself to a biscuit, before biting off the corner of a chocolate cookie. While his guests waited expectantly, James fixed his gaze at some far-off scene that only he could see. Finally, he observed very quietly, 'I knew Johnny for a long time. I published many of his novels and over the years I grew quite fond of him, but Ley Farm was the turning point. Something happened out there and he was never quite the same again.'

'How do you mean "never quite the same again"?' queried Melanie.

'Well,' explained their elderly host, 'he gradually became more and more confused. It seemed as though the place was affecting his mind in some way.' He rested his entwined hands on the edge of the table. 'You see,' he explained, 'Ley Farm is not called that for no reason. It has the distinction, if that's what you'd call it, of being positioned at the right-angle intersection of two ley lines.'

'Ley lines?' queried Melanie.

'Sorry, I should explain,' confessed the old editor. 'They are ancient trackways that have criss-crossed this country almost since before time began. They were long-considered sacred and are still purported by some to possess certain magical properties. Now, I've heard,' he continued, 'that these powers can become greatly magnified where junctions occur and emit huge amounts of unnatural energy.' James leant forward as he warmed to his topic. 'I've even heard that reality itself can become malleable and distorted for anyone after crossing such an intersection.'

Christine took a deep breath.

'As I understand it,' continued the old boy, 'the owners always entered the farm via a five-bar-gate situated at the bottom of their drive – as did most visitors and their employees. But for some reason known only to himself, John always used a small side gate and in doing so blundered right over the junction every time he visited the place.

'Now,' he added, 'what I'm about to say is, of course, pure speculation. But I know for a fact that John loved the Balearic Islands and Menorca, in particular. I also know he was a keen underwater photographer and nothing pleased him more than scuba diving in the warm shallow seas of the Mediterranean.' He stopped for a moment to smile briefly at Melanie. 'Unlike you, I'm not suggesting he jumped out of his box to join you on the beach, as you so graphically put it, but I do wonder if, perhaps, having experienced the power of the ley lines, he might have thought it possible to enjoy one last excursion in the seas he loved so well before going down to his final rest.'

Christine turned sympathetically to her friend. 'You said he seemed to disappear almost immediately after he'd spoken to you. So, perhaps, as James is suggesting, he was, in fact, granted that one last brief respite on the island.'

Melanie's response was muted, for she was now beginning to wonder if James' theorising was correct. She doubted it, but if he was right, then the only man who had ever stirred her emotionally was now forever beyond her reach by the unbridgeable factor of death. Although, if it happened once, was it possible...?

Her companion sensed her thinking and took her hand. 'I'm sorry, Melanie,' she murmured, 'but as you say, it's probably all just a coincidence.'

Indeed, a coincidence it would prove to be – but a coincidence with an ironic and strange twist.

Chapter 4

AS HE FINISHED speaking, the old editor began to collect up their cups, but, in the process, he had been covertly scrutinising Melanie. Eventually, with the tea set back on its tray, he ventured to say what he had on his mind.

'You know, it's not often an old man like me gets to have two such beautiful lady visitors.' He paused briefly and hesitated, after lifting the loaded tray, unsure whether to give voice to what else he had in mind.

Finally, it was so obvious that Christine spoke up. 'Was there something else, James?'

At this, he took the hint and slowly put the tray back on the table. 'If you'll forgive me for saying so, Melanie, I can't help but feel I've seen you somewhere before. And not just once, but on a number of occasions.' He rubbed his chin reflectively. 'Well, if it wasn't you, it was certainly someone very much like you.'

'Oh, you've probably seen us in the fashion mags,' chirped up Christine. 'We also model clothes on some of the early morning TV shows.'

Again leaning with his hands on the table, their host clicked his tongue and shook his head. Early morning TV, he assured them, did very little for him. 'Mainly,' he added, with a smile, 'because I never get up in time; privilege of old age and all that.' However, his next observation really resonated with Melanie. 'I hope you won't think I'm rude,' he ventured tentatively, 'but I was wondering whether there's any German connection in your family?' Christine immediately leant forward and exchanged glances with her friend. Unfortunately, as Melanie began to respond, there came a knock at the front door. 'Excuse me,' apologised their host.

As James left the table, Christine whispered, 'Remember how only the other day you were saying that you sometimes wondered if you had German origins?' However, her last words were almost drowned out by the welcome being extended to the new arrival.

'Hello, Tom. Come on in. There're a couple of young ladies I'd like you to meet.'

Now, the tall young man that stepped through the door certainly didn't have a straw stuck in his ear. Neither did he have any hanging from the corner of his mouth, but his West Country accent was unmistakable from the first moment.

'Ah, I didn't know you were entertaining guests, James, or I...' He paused and looked momentarily embarrassed. 'It's just that, as I were passing, I thought I'd drop in and see how you was doing.' Beneath his casual denim farmer's outfit lurked a physique of some obvious strength. In fact, his whole, rather rugged, persona seemed to quite dominate the small cottage, but seeing his uncertainty, Melanie moved to ease the situation.

'Hello, Tom,' exclaimed the blonde model in her sensuous voice as she slowly rose to welcome the newcomer. Stretching out her hand, she added, 'I'm Melanie and this is my friend, Christine.'

The old editor's visitor seemed quite overwhelmed by the sudden and unexpected exposure to such feminine glamour and it was fortunate at this point that their host intervened. 'Ladies, please allow me to introduce Mr Thomas Gardener. He's recently acquired large tracts of land in this part of the world, including my little cottage.'

Tom, who had not once taken his eyes off Melanie, smiled briefly. 'Ah. And if I be honest, I've gone and acquired far too much for me to 'andle with comfort.'

Melanie covertly studied the speaker while mentally comparing him to the mysterious author, John Grant. Physically, the two men were not dissimilar. Although this man's weather-beaten and craggy features were far from unattractive, when it came to looks, however, he couldn't hope to compete with the long-dead writer. Yet Tom exuded a simplistic warmth and sympathy that Melanie found quite appealing.

'Excuse for another brew?' piped up their host in the middle of her thoughts.

'Ah, not for me, young James, cos, as I were saying, I only just popped in to see you were okay.'

Then, turning to the two friends, he added, 'And by the looks of it, you're doing very nicely.' Finally, in his rich Cornish accent, he observed quietly, 'It be very rare I meet such beautiful young ladies and it's been a real pleasure.' Then, pausing by the front door, he nodded and flashed his West Country smile. 'Yes. It's been a real pleasure'. And, with that, he was gone.

'Well,' breathed Christine, 'you must admit, he was very pleasant.'

Melanie didn't reply, but from her expression the visitor had obviously made a mark. In any case, before she could respond, James chipped in. 'Had we decided on another brew?' he ventured, as, once more, the laden tray of dirty crockery rose from the table in readiness for their baptism in the kitchen.

'I'll go along with that,' smiled Melanie, 'but perhaps we could have black coffee instead? Oh, and very strong, please.'

Again, the tray descended.

'You know,' explained their host, while indicating the front door, 'that young man would be quite a catch for someone.'

'Well, not for this someone,' echoed Christine. 'Sorry. Although whether my friend would...?'

But Melanie shook her head.

In the meantime, Christine watched fascinated as James' hands hovered uncertainly over the forever ascending and descending tray.

'Do you know,' exclaimed the old publisher, 'that man's grandfather was a brigadier in the Korean

War? And twice mentioned in despatches. What's more, they're an extremely wealthy family.'

Christine leant back in her chair and folded her arms. 'I'm sure he would make some girl very happy, but I'm just not interested.'

James got the message and the tray rose for a final time. As he busied himself in the kitchenette converting the dirty crockery into steaming hot cups of black coffee, Christine leant across to her companion. 'I think you were more impressed with young Mr Tom than you care to admit!'

Melanie hooked her elbow over the corner of her chair while letting her gaze rove over the quaint little room. 'He was alright, I suppose – in a country sort of way.'

Halfway through her coffee, Melanie turned to James. 'Before that young man's visit, you asked me if I had any German relatives?'

For a moment, her listener looked awkward – almost as though he regretted having raised the subject. Gradually, he lowered his cup and continued to gaze down at its contents.

'As I mentioned earlier,' he began, 'I felt sure I'd seen you somewhere before and now I remember where. Come with me. I've something to show you.' But then, raising his head, he added, 'Although it could be an experience you may find a bit disturbing.'

The corners of Melanie's mouth tightened into something approaching a smile. 'I'm tougher than

I look, James,' she said. 'So, whatever it is, as the expression goes, bring it on.'

Even so, their ageing host seemed diffident about what he knew lay ahead.

The room beyond the lounge proved to be in total darkness. When James switched on the light, the reason immediately became apparent. Each wall was lined from floor to ceiling with filing cabinets.

'It's no good being a compulsive collector,' explained the old boy, 'if you haven't got somewhere to store the stuff you've collected.'

'And, er, what is all this stuff you've collected?' enquired Christine.

The answer came with a certain ring of pride and, indicating the banks of drawers, he explained how each row contained the issues of every national and major provincial newspaper since the early 1920s. 'My grandfather started keeping these and I've been doing it ever since.'

'It must be worth a fortune,' whispered Christine to her friend. However, before Melanie could reply, she saw James go straight to one of the drawers. Obviously familiar with the huge layout, he quickly removed a single newspaper and took it across to a table situated in the middle of the room.

'*The London Times*,' he explained, tapping the paper. 'Monday December 4th, 1944. It was getting towards the end of World War II and, if my memory serves me correctly,' he muttered, opening the front page, 'the article in question is just inside.'

And sure enough, there, in huge, though now slightly faded, black lettering, were the words:

REPEATED RAPE IN THE
TOWER OF LONDON

In smaller print, it reported that, although it was supposed to be the most secure place in the country, crime had still managed to be committed against the beautiful Nazi spies, Gerda Reinhardt and Monika Schneider – both of whom had been systematically abused. The article described how the guards, who had been trusted with their security, were now under close arrest and awaiting trial. It also highlighted an ironic twist in that the two women concerned had both become pregnant, thus causing their executions to be postponed pending the births – which was, effectively, a permanent reprieve because their confinements were expected to extend well beyond the end of hostilities.

Melanie was becoming impatient. 'This is very interesting, but all long before our time. So, I mean, what the hell...?'

In way of an answer, the retired editor turned the page, whereupon Melanie immediately fell silent, for there, staring out at her, was a fading monochrome photograph that might have been an image of herself. And, beneath it, a caption read:

The raped and pregnant Nazi spy, Gerda
Reinhardt. Let it be hoped that we, as
English people, are suitably ashamed of the

*diabolical treatment meted out to someone
who has been brave enough to act in such a
dangerous and courageous capacity for the
benefit of their country.*

'Now you know why I feel I've seen you before,'
stated the old man.

But his listener remained speechless as she gazed,
mesmerised, at the wartime image. Finally, however,
she spoke – albeit almost to herself. 'And I've often
wondered if I've had some kind of connection with
Germany.'

Later that evening, at their hotel, Christine found it
difficult to placate her distressed friend.

'Okay. You look like that woman in *The London
Times*. So what? A lot of people look superficially
alike.'

'Oh, no,' protested Melanie. 'There was more to
it than there just being some sort of resemblance,
for heaven's sake. That woman and I were virtually
identical. Look,' she added, 'I've long had doubts
about my parents. Yes, they're a lovely couple, but
tomorrow, sod my contract commitments, I'm
heading for home.' She crossed the hotel lounge with
a drink and plonked herself purposefully on one of
the luxurious sofas. 'A,' she stressed, 'they're not
getting any younger and I feel I've neglected them.
And B, I'm going to have it out with them about my
birth, once and for all.'

Nothing Christine could say made any difference.

There was little to distinguish one terraced house from another among the rendered grey walls of Canal Street in Shoreham. One, in particular, spelt home for Melanie and, if she was honest, it's where her heart really belonged. Somehow, all the sumptuous hotels on various assignments and the frequent invitations to differing luxuriously appointed houses were no substitute for her origins in Canal Street. This was a spontaneous visit and meant to be a complete surprise, so ignoring her key, she resorted to the bell. When her mother finally answered the door, Melanie was quick to notice how much older she seemed. Nevertheless, June's face immediately lit up at the unexpected sight of her daughter.

'Melanie!' she exclaimed excitedly, reaching up to embrace her fiercely. 'We had no idea you were coming.' Then, pulling away for a moment and with a touch of remorse, she added, 'We do miss you so.'

At this point, her daughter took the opportunity to introduce her companion. 'Mum. I'd like you to meet a dear friend of mine. This is Christine.'

Now, her mother was a warm woman and Christine found herself on the end of an almost equally enthusiastic reception. 'I've heard all about you, Christine, so it's lovely to actually meet you. But come on in and we'll have some coffee.'

Once inside the cramped little living room, Melanie began to realise just how humble her childhood had been. Everywhere she looked spoke of a shortage of money. Her parents' employment had never paid well, as demonstrated by the worn and tired-looking three-piece suite and the patches of carpet underlay that were now beginning to show.

Standing by the window and moving the faded curtains aside, Christine thought, slightly sadly, *Not much to show for two people's lifetime of work.* She gazed up and down the narrow street outside where peeling paint told a similar story. Somehow it all served to make their gleaming new Mercedes-Benz stand out incongruously among the scattering of much smaller, cheaper models.

'I know what you're thinking,' pointed out an observant Melanie, who had been settling comfortably in one of the ancient armchairs. 'But you must remember, this house and that street was my whole life for some twenty years. And I love it. And nothing, but nothing, could ever take its place.'

'Hmm...' murmured Christine as she released the curtain. 'If anyone should understand things like that, it's me – because I come from downtown Fishersgate.' Christine lowered her voice. 'Melanie, this place is your cradle. Surely you're not going to challenge your parents over something as precious as that.'

But just then, Melanie's mother came bustling in, weighed down with a tray of hot coffee. 'I'm so pleased to see you both,' she began.

'Mum,' enquired Melanie. 'Is Dad about?'

Placing the little round tray with its worn rose-petal design on a nearby table, her mother straightened up and nodded. 'Yes, love,' she replied, passing the first cup to Melanie's friend and indicating the sugar and milk jug. 'I think he's pottering about in the little shed at the back. Would you like me to ask him to come in?'

As with her mother, her father was beginning to show the passage of time and Melanie felt a pang of guilt over the infrequency of her visits. However, as he entered the room, she turned to her companion. 'Let me introduce my dad. And, Dad, this is Christine.'

'Hello,' smiled Brian, while extending his hand. 'My wife and I have heard all about your exciting exploits.'

'Well, they can be demanding, too,' replied Christine.

Finally, as they all settled down with their coffees, Brian spoke quietly; a feature Melanie remembered so well, for he'd always been a gentle soul and, as far as she could recall, had never exchanged an angry word with anyone.

'It's nice to see you, Melanie,' he continued. 'And please don't misunderstand it when I say we'd love to see you more often.'

'I know, Dad. I know. And I'm sorry. But somehow, Christine and I seem to have got swept away on a sea of glamour and fashion and, if I'm honest, a lot of false values as well.'

A slightly awkward silence ensued, punctuated only by the sound of coffee being sipped and the rattle of china cups as they descended to their saucers. Christine knew what was coming next and kept an especially discrete silence.

Finally, looking straight at her parents, Melanie asked the critical question. 'There's something I feel a desperate need to ask you both. Do you know anything about a woman called Gerda Reinhardt? I understand she was last seen in London towards the end of World War II.'

On hearing this, her father looked ashen faced while her mother appeared devastated.

Eventually, however, June spoke in a barely audible voice. 'How did you come to hear about this woman and why do you feel the need to know more about her?'

'Because,' emphasised Melanie, 'I've recently seen a photo of her in a wartime copy of *The London Times*. She was around my age and, frighteningly, could well have been my twin sister. I mean...' and, at this point, Melanie began to struggle for words, fearful of saying something that might irretrievably damage their relationship. Nevertheless, she was determined to find out the truth. 'I mean, how can two people be so alike without their being some sort of family connection?'

'It's no good, June!' exclaimed an anguished Brian. 'We've done all we can. You'll just have to tell her the truth.'

Slowly and sadly, June turned to face her daughter. 'I only know,' she said, in a subdued voice, 'what I have been told. Because you must remember I wasn't born until 1954.' She again glanced at her husband, but he only urged her to carry on. 'During the Nazi regime,' she began, 'there were two notably beautiful women. One was a singer – Marlene Dietrich, I think she was called. The other was Gerda Reinhardt.' She paused for a moment and slumped wearily in her seat, relieved to be unburdening the mental load she'd carried for so long. Finally, reaching for her cup, she drained the last of its contents. 'Anyway,' she continued, 'there was a third prominent woman associated with the Hitler regime and her name, I seem to recall, was Leni Reifenstahl. She created very successful propaganda films that were popular with Hitler. Incidentally, he was chancellor at the time. The point is, this Reifenstahl woman wanted Gerda Reinhardt to star in her greatest film – *Triumph of the Will* – and I think even some of the Nazi hierarchy tried to persuade her to take part, but she wouldn't have it. Instead, she seemed determined on espionage work, where, presumably, she felt she could make a much greater contribution to the war effort.'

At this point, Melanie took up the story that she had read in the newspaper report. 'So she came to England and landed secretly off the coast of Dover to spy on the phantom army being constructed near East Anglia, which, I think, was a decoy to divert Berlin's attention from the intended landing in the Normandy area.'

'Any chance of another cuppa, Mother?' enquired Brian. But in her distraught state, June responded snappishly, 'If you want more coffee, you'll have to get it yourself.'

At this discordant note, an almost impenetrable silence fell over the room, which was finally broken by the more tranquil Christine. 'I'll get you a cup, Brian. Err, if that's alright to call you Brian?'

To which he smiled, while turning to his daughter. 'You seem to know an awful lot about the war years considering you weren't even born until early 1981,' he observed with his working-class wisdom.

'Well,' replied Melanie, 'I made it my business to thoroughly read *The London Times* article, but more to the point, I understand this brave woman got captured and put in the Tower of London, where she was repeatedly assaulted.'

'And a disgraceful and shabby chapter it was,' echoed her father, contemptuously. 'Anyway, it resulted in both women bringing children into the world that really should never have been born. One,' he explained, 'was born dead. Which, I suppose, arguably, under the circumstances, was a blessing. But the Reinhardt woman produced a very healthy girl.'

Melanie leant forwards in her chair, her mind now fully focused, half suspecting what was coming next. Although, whatever it was had to be postponed by the arrival of Christine with Brian's coffee, while further delay ensued as he slurped it from the saucer – a long-standing habit that had always irritated both the women in his life.

'Well, then what happened?' asked Melanie, with a touch of impatience after her father had consumed half his cup.

'You must realise that, as your mother has already said, we were not aware of all the details, but, as far as we know, this child was a girl and taken away from her mother when she was only a few days old and placed in an orphanage. She was then adopted by an English couple and christened Sheila Reinhardt – although why they kept the mother's surname when the whole idea was to conceal her identity is beyond me.'

At this point, Melanie knew she was nearing a truth she'd sensed for years. Though, irritatingly, at that very moment, her mobile phone decided to sound off and, snatching it from her hip pocket, she was none too polite.

'Yes. What is it?'

Christine's mouth tightened and, rolling her eyes, she glanced at Melanie's father.

'I'm sorry if I disturbed you,' came the soft West Country-sounding voice of Tom.

Despite her initial frustration, Melanie quickly relented, because, although she'd never admit it, Tom's gentle strength seemed to offer a certain attraction. However, her unexpected caller was preparing to disengage.

'I'm sorry,' he repeated quietly. 'I'll try and call another time.'

'No, no. That's fine, Tom,' she assured him, while catching her friend's eye.

'Oh. Tom, is it?' mouthed Christine.

'Shut up!' mouthed Melanie. Then, with her eyes firmly fixed on the small panes of glass that made up the living room window, Melanie listened carefully to her caller's tentative voice. It transpired that Tom was staying in Arundel for a few days on business and had discovered a fifteenth-century hotel along the banks of the River Arun with a restaurant second to none.

'There be tables and chairs right up to the water's edge and some fantastic views over the river towards the Downs.' He paused, for the words were obviously not coming easily. 'I... ah... was wondering if, like, you'd do me the honour of having dinner with me one evening.' He stumbled on. 'It's right beautiful and I thought perhaps we could wander along the riverbank afterwards.'

The effort he was making was tangible and Melanie couldn't help but feel a tinge of sympathy as she idly watched the antics of a small spider, who had managed to ensnare a fly in the corner of one of the small windowpanes – a window, incidentally, that needed cleaning desperately.

Tom's was a tempting offer and the thought of a country walk brought back happy childhood memories of the time she'd spent with her mother exploring the local Adur waterway. Although, she didn't want to date a man on the off chance of a riverside stroll, so, after taking his number, Melanie promised to call back the following day. Meanwhile, Christine's face was a picture of curiosity.

'Oh, a date in the offing,' she grinned. 'Can I come along?'

'If – and it's a big if – I decide to go,' responded her friend, 'I'm afraid the answer's a big fat no.'

But beneath the banter lurked a hidden poignancy, for since their original meeting some four years previously, they'd always gone and done everything together.

'You sure I can't come along?' persisted Christine, with a mischievous smile. 'Just to see you don't get up to anything.'

'Look, I haven't even decided to go,' retorted Melanie. 'And as regards the chances of me getting up to anything... Well, forget it. I tell you what though, why don't you go?'

'Just as a matter of interest,' interrupted Melanie's father. 'Is this how you two always carry on?'

His daughter looked at her friend affectionately. 'Christine and I are like close sisters. We never argue, although we do wind each other up from time to time.' She paused for a moment while returning her attention to the tiny spider, who, by now, had completely consumed its prey. Finally, she observed, 'I suppose one day we will find partners, because life changes, doesn't it? That's the order of things. And sometimes I wish it wasn't.' She shrugged with a hint of melancholy. Suddenly, however, she jerked back to reality and, addressing her father, asked bluntly, 'Tell me about this Sheila Reinhardt.'

Brian glanced across at his wife, who was sitting tensely on the edge of her chair. 'We must tell her, Mother. We owe her that much.'

The situation was obviously tearing his wife apart and she fled from the room, whereupon Melanie immediately got to her feet and raced after her. Once in the kitchen, Melanie gathered her mum into her arms. 'Whatever it is that Dad has to tell me,' she assured her mother, with tears welling in her eyes, 'won't make the slightest difference to my love for you both and the wonderful childhood you provided for me.'

June broke away for a moment and looked up at Melanie through an increasingly misty vision. 'There's no need to go back in there,' she said quietly. 'I can tell you why you so resemble that photograph in *The London Times*.' She paused, before almost whispering, 'It's because she was your maternal grandmother.'

'M... my...' stuttered Melanie, which was all she could manage.

June moved across to the oven to fiddle about with things that really didn't need fiddling with and continued, 'Sheila Reinhardt worked along with me at Thompson's mushroom farm. She seemed a pleasant enough woman. In fact, we invited her back here on several occasions because she lived entirely alone in some small flat down near the estuary by Bungalow Town. You remember. It's that strip of land between the river and the sea.'

After making them both an unnecessary cup of tea, June continued, 'Anyway, one day at work, Sheila dropped a bombshell. Apparently, she'd got herself pregnant, which was a surprise really, because, although an attractive woman, in her late thirties, she had no serious boyfriends that I knew of.'

June sat down wearily while taking a sip from her cup and there, in the small kitchen, Melanie finally learned the truth. 'Melanie,' she stressed, 'you must bear in mind that your father and I did what we thought was best for everyone at the time. Sheila would have ended up a single mother, but, more importantly, she knew she was the result of rape and wanted to keep the fact from her child. Understandably, she was concerned that her baby had a clean and normal start to life with no knowledge of the past.'

'And,' completed Melanie, 'you decided to take on the responsibility yourself, which meant you had no option but to remain quiet about Gerda Reinhardt.'

Her mother nodded dumbly. Looking at Melanie, June begged, 'Please don't judge us too harshly.' Then, casting her eyes to the ground, she added, with a hint of sadness, 'Your dad and I are, of course, very happy with your success, but I do sometimes wish you'd just stayed my little daughter at home and worked at the mushroom farm, because then you would never have known anything about all this.'

It was a sentiment expressed straight from the heart and, recognising her mother's love, Melanie hugged her mother once more. 'You do realise,' her daughter reassured her, 'you will always be my loving parents.'

'And yet,' observed June, 'we see so little of you these days. I always keep a bed ready-made up for you in case... Well, it's just that I wondered if I could persuade you to stay tonight.'

It was a poignant moment, but Melanie had little

option. 'Oh, Mum. I'd love nothing better, but I must return to London and finish my current assignment. I've taken today off unofficially as it is, so God knows what trouble I'll be in when I get back tomorrow. I'm so sorry.'

Although June did her best to conceal her disappointment, the pain showed clearly in her eyes and Melanie promised faithfully she would come and stay for a few days at some time in the near future. However, with the rush of commitments and travel, "some time in the near future" was destined never to happen.

Back in the small living room, the girls prepared to say goodbye. However, unknowingly in her mother's case, it really was goodbye. Within six months of their visit, June died of a brain tumour. Melanie's only consolation was she had told her mother that she loved her. A deep sadness remained, however, knowing how much her mum had wanted her to stay for just that one night.

After a prolonged display of waving, the girls climbed into their Mercedes – albeit much to the sneering and ridicule of several local undesirables, with one lout shouting, 'Which way do you like it, love?' The vulgarity was accompanied with an appropriate hand gesture.

'Oh, let's just get the hell out of here!' exclaimed Christine, as she accelerated the automatic down the narrow street. 'How your parents put up with it, I just can't imagine. And look at the graffiti – it's everywhere.'

By this stage in their careers, the girls were staying for a few weeks in a fashionable apartment just off the Fulham Road in London. But that night, the mood was sombre.

'Ah. German extract, eh?' murmured Christine as she leant back on their designer sofa and sipped a glass of wine. 'I suppose, under the circumstances, I can appreciate your curiosity. But I can't help wondering whether it was worth putting your parents through such an ordeal. They really are a lovely couple who've only done their best for you.'

'Oh, don't,' protested Melanie. 'I feel bad enough about it already.'

'And then there's Tom,' teased her friend. 'What are you going to do about him? We're both in our early twenties now, you know, and there's not a decent man on the horizon.'

'None,' responded Melanie, 'apart from those few moments back in Menorca.'

'Huh! Well, that's a fat lot of good,' retorted her companion. 'Fancying a man that's been in the grave for some fifteen years.'

'But I wonder!' exclaimed Melanie. 'Is it really possible for such a perfect man to have been dead for so long? Yes, I know what James said about the dates and the ley lines, but when you really come to think about it, I'm not sure. I mean, you saw the man. Did he look dead or like some sort of phantom?'

'On the contrary,' smiled her companion, with a touch of envy. 'He looked every inch the real thing.'

At that moment, Christine's mobile decided

to make its presence felt. 'Hello,' she responded, with a certain lack of enthusiasm, only for her face to suddenly light up as she put her hand over the speaker. 'It's Karl, the pilot. Remember?'

'Hmm. Took his time,' replied Melanie, which, to the excited Christine, felt like a bucket of cold water.

'You're only jealous,' countered her friend.

'Sorry. Not in the slightest, dear. Anyway, I'm off to bed. Don't forget we've got the last session with the Silk face company first thing in the morning.'

Just as she reached the door, Melanie heard the tone of her friend's voice suddenly rise. 'Yes, yes, that would be lovely. We could make up a foursome, because apparently my friend's partner has found a fantastic restaurant in Arundel that overlooks the river.'

Standing in the doorway, Melanie's face was a picture as she repeatedly shook her head and formed her lips in a very decisive, 'No'.

Finally, after the phone call ended, she asked dryly, 'And how the hell are you going to get yourself out of that? Because, in case you hadn't noticed, I haven't even agreed to go out with Tom – I assume he's the partner you had in mind.'

'Oh, you'll think of something,' grinned Christine, impishly.

'I'll think of something? Look, Miss. This is your mess and you can dig your own way out of it.'

Despite all the imponderables, a week later saw two expensive cars coasting along the riverside road on their way to The Grey Hare. Just after 7pm, it was a glorious summer evening with a sinking sun that added a warm glow to a very rural setting. The hotel had originally been cut back into the cliffs. It bordered the river plain and was situated in a valley that had been forged eons ago as the last ice age had forcibly torn through the low-lying hills on its way south. All that was a far cry from the sight that greeted Melanie, as, along with Tom, she alighted from her car to gaze at the tranquil meandering river – a waterway further enhanced by great clusters of straw-coloured rushes that lined its banks and whose feathery plumes inclined to every passing breeze. On the far side of the valley, a low line of hills slumbered peacefully beneath the azure sky – almost as if daring anything or anyone to disturb them.

'Ah!' exclaimed Tom in admiration. 'I must admit you've got a right beautiful spot 'ere. Even our lovely Cornwall would be 'ard put to beat sommat like this.'

His accent grated on Melanie, and she only just managed to resist the temptation to say, 'You mean, Tom, this is a beautiful spot.' Instead, she agreed, 'Yes, isn't it lovely? And just look at that water. It's almost completely still.'

As if to prove her point and with only the slightest ripple, a group of three swans glided towards the riverbank. Obviously in search of various morsels from the riverside diners, their graceful elegance spoke of nature's design at its best. The harmony of it was very close to Melanie's heart; something she sadly missed in the hectic world of fashion.

Everything has its price and she sometimes longed for the day when she could give it all up and return to her first love: the freedom of the open countryside.

In the meadows just beyond the river, groups of cattle grazed idly in the fading brilliance, while others were merely content to lie in the grass and chew the cud. The whole rural idyll was set against a backdrop of gentle lowing. This was accompanied by a chorus of various birds perched high in the pine trees that dotted the area, while others responded from clusters of wild bushes.

At this point, they were joined by Christine and Karl.

'It's certainly a superb location,' observed the pilot, gazing around. 'That's if you can get a seat. Because, by the looks of it, everything's already been taken.' Then, turning to Tom, he asked, with an acid touch sometimes detectable in rival male voices, 'Didn't you think to book a table for us in advance?'

Tom, however, was not the kind to respond in a similar vein. 'Ah, that I did,' he replied, 'but them don't take no bookings after 7pm, so we decided to risk it on spec.'

The pilot made no reply, but his face said a thousand words and, sensing the tension, Christine was quick to pour out the oil of tranquillity. 'If we're patient, I'm sure a table will become available.'

Almost as she spoke, a nearby group of diners started making "about to move" noises – although, when they finally decided to go, the state of their table, with its piles of dirty plates and dishes, was almost enough to put them off anyway.

But then, as Christine went to sit down, she suddenly screamed.

'What is it? What's the matter?' enquired her German escort.

'There! Look,' replied the terrified woman, pointing to a container that once held some unspecified soup. 'There's something alive in that bowl!'

And sure enough, even as she spoke, a sharp-nosed insect peered over the rim. By its vicious intermittent buzzing, Karl instantly recognised it as a hornet and raised his fist for the death blow. However, Tom again showed the quality of his character and intervened.

'Ah. I'll deal with that. The little wee fella has all the right to live the same as the rest of us.' And he carefully took the bowl to a nearby bush and gently shook the insect free; free to fly away and complete the cycle of life granted to it, at least in Tom's opinion, by God.

As he returned, the table was being cleared by two young and obviously overworked waitresses. Melanie observed quietly, 'That was a very humane thing to do, Tom. I admire that. It's a sensitive trait you don't often see in men.'

'Yes. That's not something I'd have liked to have done,' exclaimed Christine with a shudder. But then, turning to Tom, she suggested, 'Look. The staff are very busy at the moment, so why don't you and I get the drinks from the bar in the meantime?'

Their departure left Melanie alone with Karl for the first time and she leant across the now clear table.

'Am I right in remembering that your grandfather flew one of the Junkers 88 bombers during the last war?' Her move had brought the low sunlight directly into her eyes and she responded by snapping on her designer dark glasses.

'*Ja*, that is correct,' he nodded, lapsing partly back into his native language. For a moment, an uncharacteristic look of sadness passed across his handsome features, before he added, 'He also flew Heinkels and occasionally piloted Me109 fighters.' Karl paused before adding, 'I never knew him, but he must have been a very brave man.' He reached for the saltshaker and toyed with it between his forefinger and thumb. Then, frowning, he continued, 'You know, it takes quite a lot of courage to fly the large commercial airliners in peacetime. But what it must have been like at night, with the ground flak and night fighters to contend with, beggars the imagination. Certainly,' he confessed, 'it would have been far too much for me.'

'And what happened to your grandfather?' enquired Melanie. 'Did he survive the war?'

'No, no,' Karl replied in a matter-of-fact voice, while still fiddling with the salt dispenser. 'He got killed. It was in 1941 during a night raid on the London Docks. According to one of the pilots who did make it back, my grandfather's plane got caught in the crossbeam of searchlights and was shot down in a ball of flames.'

'Oh, what a terrible way to die!' exclaimed his horrified listener.

The German paused to gaze out across the tranquil river. 'Such a different world,' he added quietly. Then, looking straight at Melanie, he observed unexpectedly, 'You know, human beings were given a wonderful and incredibly beautiful home we call earth, but from time to time we've turned it into a hell. As I said, I never knew my grandfather and it's a great sadness to me that he's got no known grave. He ended his days that night somewhere in the inferno of the Thames Estuary.'

Moved by this obvious sorrow, Melanie did something quite out of keeping and reached across the table to touch his forearm. 'I'm sorry, Karl,' and she followed his gaze as he continued to look out over the waterway. 'The lives of millions were destroyed or bereaved in that war,' she murmured sympathetically. 'And strangely enough, I only recently discovered how even I have been affected.'

'Oh?' he queried, finally leaving the salt cellar to its own devices. 'How's that?'

'Well, I'd had my suspicions for some time, but before I go into detail, tell me, have you ever heard of a woman called Gerda Reinhardt?'

The pilot frowned again. 'It rings a bell,' he said, finally. Then added, 'I seem to think she was a contemporary to the likes of Greta Garbo and other goddesses of the silver screen.'

'She was more than that,' insisted Melanie. 'Did you know she rated as one of the most beautiful women during the whole of the Third Reich era? Anyway,' she continued, 'to cut a long story short, she offered her services for espionage – probably thinking her beauty might seduce men into parting with wartime secrets. But it was a costly decision,' Melanie added, 'for she lost not only her freedom, but became pregnant. And I'm the direct result. You see, she was my grandmother. So, in fact, I'm part German. I've long had doubts about my background and I finally got the truth a week or so back. I hated doing it, because my parents have always been so good and loved me like their own flesh and blood, but I just had to know.'

'You mean they adopted you?' concluded her listener. 'And never told you?' He smiled a mischievous smile. 'So that's why you're so beautiful. Gerda Reinhardt's granddaughter? Well, well. If that doesn't beat all.'

She looked briefly embarrassed, but then added, 'Being beautiful is a gift, but it's transitory and fades.'

'Ah. Holding hands with my date, are we?' came Christine's unexpected and slightly amused voice.

Melanie had been too engrossed to notice the approach of Tom and her friend. 'Sorry,' she smiled. 'It was purely a gesture of commiseration. Nothing more. Karl was telling me how tragically his grandfather died during the last war.'

That summer evening left Melanie with fond memories, the most enjoyable of which had been the stress-free ramble along the river after their meal. Blackberry bushes had grown in abundance by the waterway and at that time of year, their tempting small shiny pipped fruit seemed everywhere. It was too much for Melanie, who irritated her companions by constantly stopping to pick at particularly juicy bunches – although Tom, always the consummate gentleman, was the first to use his height advantage to bring the inaccessible ones within her reach.

Somehow, the whole experience had reminded Melanie of the times spent with her mother exploring the banks of the Adur; a happy childhood now gone forever. *Was childhood the best time of my life?* she sometimes wondered. The answer always came back as a resounding: *Yes.*

Chapter 5

SEVERAL HEAVY COMMITMENTS on the catwalks of Paris over a number of weeks followed that pleasant summer evening in England. The girls had rented an ultra-contemporary flat in a fashionable area that overlooked the Seine and Notre-Dame Cathedral.

After one particularly punishing day, Christine poured them both a glass of Burgundy and sank down wearily to gaze out of the huge window, with its panoramic view of the famous river and the twin towers of the holy centre – a place that had been the focus of French worship for so many centuries. Finally, after laying her head back on the cushions, she observed, 'It's your birthday next week.'

'I believe you're right,' echoed an equally weary Melanie. 'Although I wish it wasn't.'

'You know,' observed her friend, 'some people our age are thinking of getting married and having a family – which is alright, I suppose. If you want one! But,' she added philosophically, 'this champagne lifestyle of ours won't last forever.'

'To be perfectly honest,' responded Melanie, 'as you know, there're few men that interest me. It's either that or, perhaps, I'm just undersexed! All show and nothing to back it up.'

Christine reluctantly abandoned the comfort of her seat in order to top up their drinks. 'But what about Tom?' she countered. 'Surely he's man enough for any woman. Not only that, he's rich.' She shook the wine bottle vigorously to emphasise the point. 'You'd have a completely comfortable life with him. And more than that – he fancies you something rotten.'

'The only trouble there,' explained Melanie, with a degree of false patience, 'is that I don't fancy him rotten. In fact, I hardly fancy him at all.' She held up a restraining hand. 'I know, I know. He's thoughtful, gentle and kind to small dumb insects. But he's a yokel, Christine. Straight from the farmyard down Dorset way.'

'What you really mean,' Christine replied pointedly, 'is he's not that dead author fella you're holding a candle for. For heaven's sake, you've only ever seen him once.' Collapsing back on her seat, she added in a hopeless voice, 'How you can remain fixated with a man you barely know and with whom you've never exchanged more than half a dozen words is beyond me.'

'It may not make sense,' replied Melanie. 'But that's the way it is.'

Christine shrugged at the futility of their conversation. 'I mean, what are you going to do, for goodness' sake? Go and dig him up and passionately express your feelings to his corpse?'

'The man I saw in Menorca,' insisted Melanie, 'was no corpse. I don't care what that antiquated old editor, James, said.' But then added thoughtfully, 'It's just possible the answer to the mystery could be with the ley lines at that farm. You know, the setting for the story, *Straw Hat*.' She stretched her elegant body to its fullest extent on the settee and allowed her abundant hair to cascade over the armrest. 'You remember,' she added, 'how that old man was rabbiting on about the eighth of certain months and intimated that the ley line crossover might have afforded the author an extra day. Well,' she continued, 'I was wondering...'

'Are you by any means going to say,' her friend almost shouted, while sitting bolt upright, 'that you are contemplating crossing those ley lines in some vain hope of finding that author in the same way? You're mad to even think such a thing. Apart from anything else, it smacks of the occult – something my parents would have avoided like the plague. If you meddle in the dark forces of this world, don't think any good will come of it. Because it won't.'

Christine could have had no means of knowing the dire implications of her warning, but she had delivered her opinion with such vigour that it momentarily left Melanie speechless. Finally, however, her companion said sadly, 'He was the only man who ever moved me, and I genuinely believe I could have fallen in love with him.' She paused and reached for the French magazine, *Fashion Paris*, and began idly flicking through its glossy pages, all of which were filled with scantily clad models in the latest designer outfits. She looked at her friend. 'Did you see you're on the front cover this month?' Then, in a sudden wave of despair, she added, 'I suppose I'll just have to be content to never see him again.'

Christine hopelessly rolled her eyes as she felt her mobile sounding off. 'Hello,' she responded quietly. Then, covering the phone with her hand, she mouthed at Melanie, 'It's Karl. I don't know how, but he's managed to trace us here and wants me to join him in the bar downstairs.' She rushed to the nearest mirror in a desperate attempt to restore some semblance of order to her dense mane of hair.

Whenever Christine entered any sort of public venue, there were always men who stared. It was a familiar fact of life to which she'd become accustomed. However, she couldn't avoid a surge of pleasure at the pilot's reaction, for his face immediately lit up upon catching sight of her.

'You must think I'm stalking you,' he confessed as he stepped away from the bar. 'Which, in a way, I suppose I am!'

Christine then did something quite unusual for her. Taking both his hands, she looked up into his eyes and whispered, 'Well, I'm not complaining, am I?'

There can be moments so rare and precious as to seem almost magical. For some people, it never happens, while for others it might be a once-in-a-lifetime occurrence. And this was one of those occasions for Christine. The one moment that she instinctively knew would change her life forever.

If I should spend my whole life through
And yet miss that one transcending moment
Then, surely, I would have to ask
What was the purpose of my journey in the
first place?

The next second, her universe exploded into a myriad of colour and joy as he gathered her into his arms with a kiss she thought would never end.

When they finally parted, Karl noticed a man sitting at the bar apparently watching their every move. German to the core, he turned and marched over to demand what he was staring at. However, if Karl had been entertaining any thoughts of intimidation, he was wasting his time, for the offender was well built and carried a quiet confidence with it. At first, when challenged, there was no response, but when the man did speak, it was obvious he was highly educated and well able to express himself.

'I can assure you,' he began quietly, 'that I was not staring in the sense you have in mind. But, as I'm sure you must be aware, your companion is a very beautiful young lady, which, incidentally, makes you a lucky man.' He smiled briefly. 'However, if I may point something out? Beauty is not a personal possession and is to be enjoyed by everyone. Therefore, is it really so terrible if the beauty of your friend occasionally lifts someone's spirits?'

He shrugged. 'Anyway, if I've caused any offence, I apologise. But, again, I assure you there was nothing sensual involved.'

For a moment, the man's logic disarmed the commercial pilot and he nodded. '*Ja*, you make for a fair case – but beware. Other men may not be so tolerant.' He turned sharply and joined an anxiously waiting Christine.

'What was all that about?' she began.

'Nothing. It was nothing,' Karl explained. 'Besides, I have far more important things to discuss with you.' And he indicated one of the booths situated opposite the bar. 'But first. Please. What drink can I get for you?'

'Would a small G&T be okay?' she smiled.

Finally sitting opposite each other, Karl leant forwards with his arms resting on the small dividing table. 'I've been thinking,' he began, in his direct, pragmatic way. 'I'll be thirty-five years old this year and I'm still not married.' He frowned slightly. 'I don't even have a steady girlfriend – I believe is the expression.' Filled with curiosity, Christine studied his face over the rim of her glass and wondered what was coming next. She didn't have long to wait.

Despite his intelligence and physical presence, subtlety was not among Karl's attributes and, without any forewarning, he suddenly exclaimed, 'I think, therefore, I would like you to be my fiancée.' At this point, he reached into his tunic pocket to withdraw something that he kept concealed in the palm of his hand. 'You'll need to wear this to show we are a couple.' Then, opening his hand, crystal rays of light sparkled and reflected from the diamonds of the most exquisite gold ring Christine had ever seen.

She opened her mouth to respond, but, in the face of such blatancy, words failed her. Finally, however, after taking a section of her auburn hair and tossing it vigorously back over her shoulder, she exclaimed, 'Karl! To say the least, don't you think you're being a bit premature? We hardly even know each other.'

Christine's words were a smokescreen – to conceal that she was overjoyed with excitement. Ever since first seeing Karl during their flight to Menorca, she had been deeply impressed by his looks, his abundant self-confidence and his job.

'You mean,' he said, 'you think I'm rushing things?'

'Er, well, just a bit,' she managed.

'But why wait?' he objected. 'You obviously find me attractive, and you are one of the most beautiful girls I've ever seen, so...'

'Karl,' she gasped, with her mind still reeling. 'I don't know what to say.' In actual fact, she knew exactly what to say. It would have been something along the lines of, 'Of course. I'd be ecstatic to be your fiancée and wear this lovely ring.' But personal dignity and a sense of propriety dictated a more cautious approach. So, she reached over to take his hand and whispered, 'I feel very honoured by your proposal. But, seriously, I really do need a little time to think it over.'

114

His handsome features clouded over. 'So, you will not be my fiancée then?'

In his direct world, she had refused him, and Christine began to feel her initial euphoria becoming tinged with impatience. 'Karl!' she exclaimed. 'That's not what I said, and you must realise I can't make a decision that will affect the rest of my life on the spur of the moment. But there's also something else.'

'What else can there be?'

'Well,' she teased, 'if you get me another G&T, I'll tell you.'

Then, with the required drink in hand, Christine did one of her favourite tricks and gazed seductively over the rim of the glass with her large brown eyes. 'You must remember,' she purred, 'that when we first met, you only ever had eyes for Melanie. So, there's something I need to tell you in absolute confidence to help you understand my feelings.' She paused for a moment to sip her gin and tonic. Then, putting the drink down, she added, 'You see, Karl, Melanie is the best friend I've ever had. If anything, we're closer than sisters, and yet...'

'And yet?' he echoed, with a puzzled expression. 'And yet, what?'

'Well,' she began hesitantly. 'I first saw her at a seaside beauty contest that she won outright, while I was quite pleased to come second.' She shook her head. 'I know it sounds strange, but somehow, and in some way, it's always left me feeling slightly second-best where Melanie's concerned. In our world of modelling, I sense that men focus on her first. I suppose it's silly really, but that's how it affects me and makes me wonder if she would pose a threat to any future relationship we might have.'

'I see.' He nodded. 'I seem to have heard the expression somewhere that gentlemen always prefer blondes.'

'And she's blonde,' emphasised Christine. 'And it's quite genuine.'

He again nodded, while at the same time changing the subject back to the ring. 'This has been in the von Jörgensen family for more generations than is known.' Then, taking her hand and pressing the ring gently into her palm, he murmured, 'While you consider what I have proposed, will you at least keep it as a reminder of my sincerity. That ring,' he added, 'is more than just another piece of jewellery, but a token of my honourable intentions. And,' he smiled, 'they are not directed at Melanie.'

Unable to resist such honesty, she reached over and covered his hand with her own. 'I will take the greatest care of it,' she promised. 'Now, on a more mundane note, I must get to bed. I've a long day tomorrow.' She kissed her forefinger and pressed it against his lips. 'Goodnight, Karl,' she whispered. 'You've made it a surprising and wonderful day. I'll be in touch real soon, I promise.' As she reached the foot of the stairs and turned to wave, she thought Karl looked a slightly forlorn figure sitting there alone.

By the time Christine reached their apartment, bursting to tell Melanie her news, it was a bit of an anti-climax, because her friend had long since retreated to the comfort zone of bed. In the event, this was a wise decision, for the following day saw an early morning modelling commitment at the prestigious Ritz hotel in central Paris – probably the most fashion-conscious part of the capital. Then, at 2pm, they were due to take off for Heathrow, which would allow for their appearance on an evening television show in London.

It was now extremely late and Christine was very tired. She just hoped she would be equal to the heavy schedule that lay ahead, while at the same time looking fresh and relaxed as the world of eternal youth always demanded.

Chapter 6

'ARE YOU SURE he actually asked you to marry him?' queried a surprised Melanie. They were now staying in an upmarket hotel near the ITV studios. It was the following evening, after Karl's effective proposal and the first opportunity she'd had to hear Christine's news. 'You mean, he actually asked you to marry him?' she repeated incredulously.

'Well, there's no need to sound so shocked,' protested her friend. 'People do get married, you know.'

'Yes, but not in our world,' laughed Melanie. 'It's all about cohabitation and then moving on to the next partner.'

In response to her friend's cynicism, Christine showed her Karl's ring. 'I don't think so in this case,' she murmured. 'I genuinely believe he's sincere. Strange, isn't it? How we were talking about marriage and families only the other day. And then, out of the blue...'

Melanie suddenly looked tired and deflated as she slowly sat down. 'If this is really what you want, and you think it will make you happy, then, of course, no one would be more pleased than me.' Suddenly, looking up at her friend and with a slightly sad expression, she observed quietly, 'You know, we've been together a long time. Yes, there have been occasions when it's been very demanding, but it's also been very good fun.'

'I know what you're trying to say,' interrupted Christine. 'Any marriage would put an end to our way of life.'

'Well, it would, wouldn't it?' protested Melanie.

Christine glanced down at the floor. 'Yes,' she admitted finally. 'I'm afraid it probably would.'

'There's also something else,' murmured Melanie, with a slight break in her voice. 'I've grown very fond of you over the years and would miss you terribly.'

Christine knew her friend would never say such a thing lightly and rushed across the room to reassure and embrace her. 'Look, I haven't even made a definite decision yet. And even if I do, I would never allow it to interfere with what we've got.'

The words were warm, and Melanie knew they were well meant. However, deep down, she also knew the practicalities of married life and having a family would invariably force them apart. The thought left her feeling sad and cold inside as she faced the brutal truth that life changes – no matter how hard you might try to resist it.

The following late afternoon, Karl called round to collect Christine, which left Melanie alone in the apartment and with no protection from her inner anguish. For years, the two girls had been constant companions and rarely apart, but now a crack had appeared to endanger their togetherness. In addition, the post that morning delivered the possibility of a second, and far greater, threat to their relationship. In her hand, Melanie held a large buff-coloured envelope. Crossing to the window, she withdrew the contents to peruse them for the umpteenth time. They contained an offer that most young women in her position would have died for. The letter was headed "United America Film Productions" and it read:

> *Dear Miss Jordan,*
>
> *The corporation consider you would be an ideal female lead to act with Alan Ford in the forthcoming film Troubled Waters. Should you be interested, we can arrange a screen test, but we must emphasise that this has to be completed within two weeks of the date of this correspondence.*

The letter then concluded with details, email addresses and how the necessary arrangements could be made.

Melanie raised her eyes from the unexpected letter and let her gaze drift out through the window. The River Thames wound far away towards the Kent town of Gravesend. Christine had already told her that somewhere out there, Karl's grandfather had paid the ultimate price for Hitler's folly. It was late October now and a deep grey mist had begun to roll in from the distant estuary to give the whole view a damp and depressing atmosphere. Melanie always loved the springtime when everything was bursting with new life – so different from what she saw now. Yet, at this moment, it ironically matched her own downbeat mood. She didn't want her glamorous lifestyle with her friend to change. The idea of travelling alone to the various fashion venues seemed unthinkable, while the thought of going to America alone...

Certainly, had it not been for Christine's support, Melanie would never have dreamt of approaching the top modelling agency in the first place. Her disposition had been largely shaped by a quiet home background, where, as an only child, she had been loved, and her joy in the freedom of nature – and, indeed, the joy of freedom itself – had been nurtured. Therefore, to have become involved in the somewhat alien glare and glamour of the fashion industry on her own would have been out of the question. Hence, her friend's recent news now threw her into a panic.

At the back of Melanie's mind lingered a distant, yet persistent, guilt over the neglect of her parents, who had provided her with such a loving childhood – a childhood she would have given anything to re-experience for just one day. The current trauma, together with the unhappiness over her parents and the uncertainty of the future, were combining to bring her close to breaking point. She broke the tension by an outburst of anger. Screwing the American letter into a tight ball, she hurled it into the far corner of the room with all her strength. Then, reaching for her cape, she draped it round her shoulders and, with her heavy long blonde hair falling free, she strode towards the apartment door.

The hotel at which they were currently staying was a luxuriously appointed establishment, with a number of restaurants and bars that would have graced the best ocean liners. Entering one of the larger facilities, Melanie made for the ornate counter. Normally accompanied by Christine, she was now alone and presented an enticing proposition. Still in her early twenties, Melanie moved effortlessly on long shapely legs, which, combined with her curvaceous figure and beautifully sculptured features, had always been a magnet for the male gender. Only her expression marred this overall feminine vision and, perching herself on one of the bar stools, she demanded a double whisky. The smartly dressed barman, whose uniform reflected the luxury of his surroundings, immediately responded – albeit with the merest twitch of his dark eyebrows. However, the twitch became more distinctive as Melanie sank the liquor in a single go before immediately ordering a second.

Strangely, the effect Melanie had on men had always left her with a certain cynicism. She was only too aware of her power to arouse them – a fact, she once confided to Christine: 'I've got it. They want it. But they're not having it.'

However, this attitude had carried a fatal flaw, because it had been inadvertently projected onto the one man she could have loved. And, as she sat there, she could see him once again in her mind's eye – fresh from his swim in the Mediterranean and with the seawater still dripping from his broad chest. She closed her eyes as she downed the third double, and, again, she could hear his voice.

'Good book?'

She bitterly remembered how, initially, she'd felt like telling him to mind his own business and how, after his gracious self-introduction, she had somehow managed to let him slip away. Passing her glass over the bar for a refill, Melanie so longed for the opportunity to live those moments just once more. But, those precious five minutes in her life were gone and gone forever.

'Can I pay for that?' came a sudden, unexpected male voice. Melanie turned and found herself looking at a handsome middle-aged man. Smartly dressed and in a dark evening suit complete with a black bow tie, he was the kind of man a lot of women would have found very attractive. Unfortunately, in her profession, Melanie had seen thousands of his kind: predatorial men willing to chance their arm for a fling with a younger woman. If Melanie had learned one thing in the fashion business, it was worldly wisdom and she responded accordingly.

'No, thanks. Get lost!' she snapped in a slurred voice. It sounded rude. It was meant to be, for she felt bitter and sad.

However, the black bow tie was not so easily deterred, and in her alcohol-fuelled misery and in a repetition of her reaction in Menorca, Melanie lashed out and caught the man right across the left side of his face.

'Why don't you just bugger off and leave me alone?' she screamed, as he staggered back, clutching at the vivid weal on his cheek.

In this kind of upmarket hotel, such behaviour was totally inappropriate and two uniformed barmen immediately closed in.

'I'm sorry, madam, but I must ask you to leave the bar area immediately. And I should also warn you that the management may terminate your residency here.'

Apart from the odd glass of wine, Melanie had virtually been a non-drinker, so the effect on her brain at suddenly being exposed to so much alcohol had devastating consequences. While being almost unable to stand, her verbal response was both uncharacteristic and abusive.

'And if I don't? What the fuck are you going to do about it?'

The hotel staff, whose outfits were designed to blend harmoniously with the ambient atmosphere, were really no better than smartly dressed bouncers, while, needless to say, practically every other client in the restaurant area was, by this stage, agog. It's strange how people love a little distraction, especially the negative kind and at someone else's expense. The bouncers had been carefully selected and trained. So, even in the face of Melanie's provocative behaviour, they initially maintained a veneer of propriety.

'I'm sorry, madam,' insisted the taller of the two, 'but if you refuse to leave, we'll have no alternative but to forcibly escort you back to your apartment.'

At this, Melanie sneered, while still hanging on to the bar rail, 'I'd bloody like to see you try.'

Half an hour previously, Christine and Karl had returned earlier than expected. They'd been to the theatre, but it had proved so boring they'd walked out halfway through.

'Hi, Mel. It's us,' she called out as they entered the apartment. But the silence that greeted them was deafening and she turned to her companion. 'I don't know where the hell she is. I thought she'd be staying in for a quiet drink and the telly.'

Glancing round the main lounge area, Karl spotted the screwed-up letter that Melanie had discarded earlier that evening. He spread it out on a cushion and called to Christine.

'Hey. Take a look at this. It seems like some kind of invitation for your friend to take part in an American film. Wow!' he exclaimed. 'What an opportunity. Why on earth would she treat it like this?'

Christine, however, knew how her friend's mind worked. 'Melanie,' she explained, 'might look very glamorous and worldly, but it's a veneer. In reality, she comes from a quiet home background and feels more at home in the countryside.'

'Well, what on earth is she doing in frontline modelling and all the strains that go with it?' questioned a slightly puzzled Karl.

'It's easy for her, Mister Pilot,' retorted her companion. 'Easy, that is, as long as I'm along for support.' She glanced briefly at the letter. 'I must admit, I had no idea about this. Although how she would face the prospect of Hollywood, I can't begin to imagine. Especially if she thought I wouldn't be with her.' Suddenly, Christine looked worried as she glanced at Karl. 'I know she took it badly when I mentioned about us yesterday. And now this.' She looked thoughtful for a moment before adding, 'If Melanie really wanted to take up this offer, I'd have to go as well. I know it's not what you'd have liked, but...'

He smiled and shrugged in response. 'I'm hardly in a position to object. You haven't even agreed to be my fiancée yet.'

At this, she rushed across the room and, while still clutching the crumpled letter, threw her arms around his neck.

'Do I really need to say yes?' she murmured, while burying her head into his shoulder.

After several moments, he pulled away and gazed at her intently. 'You mean that? I mean, really mean it?'

The warmth of her smile and the shine in her eyes told him all he needed to know, and for some time they just stood holding hands, briefly lost in their own exquisite world.

Finally, Christine observed, 'I'm concerned about Melanie. It's just not like her to go off on her own.'

'Is there anywhere she might be?' asked Karl.

'Hmm. The only possibility I can think of,' mused Christine, 'might be the bar in the restaurant downstairs. She doesn't normally drink, but I just wonder. Anyway, come on. Let's get down there.'

As they entered the communal area of the hotel, Karl caught sight of the two barmen escorting the struggling and protesting Melanie towards the entrance. Karl was a proud German for whom the mists of two world wars had never entirely dispersed. He also epitomised that sense of Saxon competence and direct action that had helped make his home country a great nation. Moreover, Melanie was part German, and his fury knew no bounds at the sight of her being physically manhandled by two Englishmen – the old enemy.

Standing fully six feet three, Karl ploughed his way across to the bar where he grabbed the nearest offender by the shoulder and spun him round. Then, swinging from knee level, Karl smashed his right fist against the man's jaw, which sent him falling back and clutching at the bar before finally collapsing to the floor in an inert heap.

Stunned by the ferocity of the attack, the second barman lost no time in releasing his hold on the model and standing well back. Meanwhile, the normally sedate atmosphere of the bar – a place frequented by bow ties and smart dresses – was in a state of uproar and as Karl swept the unstable Melanie up in his arms, the man who had originally approached her made his voice heard.

'I recognise you, sir. You're one of the World Airways pilots and that was a very serious assault. I wouldn't be at all surprised...'

But Karl was in no mood for niceties. 'I couldn't care less what you'd be surprised at or not, old man. But I tell you this. Nobody, but nobody, manhandles this young woman while I'm around.' And with that, he made for the exit with the befuddled Melanie still in his arms.

Finally, back in their apartment, Karl gently lowered Melanie onto the sofa. He straightened out her legs and asked Christine to hand him a blanket.

'The best thing is to just let her sleep it off.'

'I only hope you don't get into trouble over all this,' Christine replied. 'Or, worse still, lose your job.'

'Oh, don't worry. There're not that many qualified pilots about,' he assured her.

As he spoke, there came a sharp knock on the door. When Christine opened it, she found herself confronted by someone she immediately recognised as the hotel manager. Rotund, bald but very smart in his pinstriped suit, he looked every inch the man for his position. What really caught her attention were his heavy and sagging spider-veined jowls. After the debacle in the bar, Christine was not really surprised to see him, while her impact on him was almost seismic. The manager gazed at her auburn hair tied loosely to hang down one side of her face, which, together with her seductive eyes and legs, personified the eternal femme fatale. What was more, Christine knew it and, unlike her friend Melanie, was not averse to exploiting the fact.

'Can I be of assistance?' she asked in a silky voice.

Obviously backfooted, the man, nevertheless, did his best to maintain some semblance of dignity. 'I'm afraid,' he began, pompously, 'that after the affray downstairs tonight, which I understand was caused by the lady who shares this apartment, I must ask you both to leave first thing in the morning. It's a serious matter,' he added. 'One of my senior assistants has been badly concussed by an associate of yours and has been hospitalised. I must also warn you that this won't be the end of the matter, by any means.'

At the manager's reference, Karl immediately made his presence felt. 'If you're talking about me,' he retorted, 'then I must point out that those two thugs you call barmen are little more than common bouncers. I do know, because I saw that goon I smacked recently engaged in a fracas outside the Icon nightclub in Ship Street. So, don't give me that crap about him being a senior barman.' He then angrily took a step closer, but the manager clearly possessed a strong sense of self-preservation and wisely backed away. 'I'll also tell you this,' snarled Karl. 'The way they were manhandling my friend, they're lucky they didn't both get a damn good thrashing.'

The manager had heard enough and made a hasty retreat.

'Well!' exclaimed Christine as she closed the door. 'You don't mince your words, do you?' Then, she added with a smile, 'I can see I'll have to be very good if I'm to be your fiancée.'

At this, he took her in his arms. 'Nobody, but nobody, could be safer with me than you,' he assured her.

Although she smiled again, a slight shadow flickered in the back of her mind, for, not only in the fashion business but also life in general, she'd heard many accounts of domestic violence. She just hoped and wondered...

Their stay at the present hotel had been brought to an abrupt end, although their current commitment to the early morning ITV programme was far from over. Fortunately, hotels abounded in this particular part of the city and the next morning saw the two friends moving into The Darchester, which was a mere stone's throw from the television studios. And it was here that Christine was to experience the greatest shock of her life.

Chapter 7

IT WAS RARE for the two girls to work separately, but on this occasion Melanie's contract expired three weeks before her friend's and she had to fly straight to Manchester to again help promote the facial cream, Silk. But it was a move that would potentially foreshadow a tragic end.

By now, Karl and Christine had become very close and saw as much of each other as possible between various commitments. Moreover, she was wearing the beautiful diamond ring – a fact of which Melanie was only too aware, and it was having an increasingly depressing effect on her.

Where is my man? she would ask herself bitterly. *Rotting in the grave.* After work and alone in a hotel room, she dwelt on her own unhappiness more and more.

Meanwhile, one evening back at The Darchester, Christine and Karl were enjoying a quiet drink and discussing the future. A future that, with their varied careers, seemed difficult to reconcile.

'Look,' Karl stated, perhaps a little unsympathetically, 'you don't have to work. My salary with World Airways would be more than adequate to keep us both in comfort.'

'And what am I supposed to do?' retorted Christine. 'When you're away on long-haul flights for days at a time? And that's not to mention Melanie. You seem to forget how close we are and that we've worked together for years.'

The room fell silent for a moment as Karl got up and crossed to the window, where he stood with his hands clasped behind his back before observing, finally, 'You can't live a life forever ruled by Melanie. I mean, how's it all going to end? Have you ever thought of that? I'll tell you how it's going to end. There'll be two bitter old spinsters living together and wishing they'd done something different.' Then, turning from the window, he continued, 'Now is the time and the opportunity to do that something different. Can't you see that?'

Christine could see it and she could see it only too well. But it solved nothing.

'Look,' he suggested suddenly, 'I work almost entirely out of Heathrow and a lot of your assignments are in the London area, anyway. Surely, if we set up home in the city, we could make it work. I mean, you don't have to do all those long-term commitments in places like Rome and Paris. You could at least cut down on that a bit.'

As Christine started to reply, there came a sharp knock at the door, reminiscent to the one at the previous hotel. 'I suppose you haven't whacked

132

anybody else lately, have you!' she observed, looking at her companion with a slight smile. Karl smiled back and shook his head, but as she opened the door the sight that met her gaze sent her into a fit of uncontrollable screaming. She backed away from the entrance. Her hand clasped over her mouth, Christine kept repeating, 'No, no. It can't be. You're dead. You've been dead for years!'

Alarmed by her reaction, Karl rushed to the doorway to find a man standing there, but this was no ordinary man. Probably in his late thirties, he stood at least an inch taller than himself. He was also noticeably well built, with thick, dark blond hair that hung low over his forehead.

Initially ignoring the visitor, who was a complete stranger, Karl spun round to the distraught and sobbing Christine. 'What is it? What's the matter?'

'That man,' she cried almost hysterically, while pointing at the doorway, 'is supposed to have died years ago. Yet Melanie and I saw him briefly on a beach in Menorca. He claimed to be the author of a book I'd bought called *Straw Hat*.'

'Sorry,' exclaimed Karl, 'but I don't understand. So, he's an author. But what gives you the idea he's dead? And that's even presupposing he's the same man you saw originally.'

Christine risked a quick look past Karl's shoulder. 'It's him alright,' she insisted. 'I'd know him anywhere.'

The unexpected caller took a step forward. 'Look,' he began in his deep voice, 'if I could just explain.'

But Karl held up a restraining hand while repeating his question to Christine. 'Why do you think this man's dead?'

'Because,' she tried to explain in the same broken voice, 'Melanie wanted to contact him, but the retired editor of the firm who published his book assured us he'd died some fifteen years previously.'

'Well,' argued Karl, 'he couldn't have been dead and alive on a beach all at the same time, could he?'

'It wasn't as simple as that,' she protested. 'Although, when I think about what the man said, the sillier it sounds.'

'Well, what did the old chap say?' urged the increasingly exasperated Karl.

At this point, the new arrival tried again. 'Look. There's a perfectly simple explanation for all this.'

However, if there was, Karl didn't want to hear it from him and insisted it came from Christine. 'Well, James Chronestead – that was the old editor's name – said that the author,' and she again indicated the man at the door, 'set the story of his novel *Straw Hat* in a real location where two ley lines intersected. And when he died, he'd stipulated that his cortege should stop by this intersection.' She paused to assess the effect this was having on Karl, who urged her to continue. 'Well,' she went on, 'James said the funeral took place on the eighth of the month and, by coincidence, it was also the eighth when we saw him. Now,' she recalled, 'to be fair, the old editor never said it in so many words, but definitely implied the ley lines might have empowered him with the extra day in Menorca.' She shrugged. 'I know it sounds a nonsense, but what other explanation can there be?'

Karl's reaction, however, was not as incredulous as she might have expected. 'I'm aware of the reputed effects of ley lines,' he admitted, 'and that in some cases they have been associated with occult powers. But as regards...' At this point, he turned to their visitor. 'Come on in and let's hear your version.'

The newcomer moved forwards slowly and, as he did so, the light caught his steely eyes. He wore a grey suit. The jacket was unbuttoned and hung open to reveal a close-fitting white sports vest. *This is an action man*, thought Karl, now seeing him close-up. Christine could well understand why he was the only man who had ever interested Melanie.

Before even inviting him to sit down, Karl demanded, 'Well, what is your explanation? How can you be dead and standing here at the same time? Also, I'd like to know the purpose of your visit, because you've terrified my fiancée – something I don't take to very kindly.'

At first, the visitor made no reply, but just stared back. Finally, he began, in his low voice, 'By your accent, I'd say you're German.' Karl didn't like his tone and took a step forward, which made Christine uneasy because she had already witnessed what her companion was capable of, and in the tense atmosphere that followed, it looked as though all hell was about to break loose. So, standing between the two men, she faced the newcomer.

'Won't you just tell us why you're here? There's really no need for any unpleasantness, because I genuinely believed you were dead.' Christine's gentle tone and softer feminine presence made the man visibly relax, thereby proving the ancient maxim: "A soft answer turneth away wrath, but grievous words stir up anger".

'I'm looking for a woman called Melanie and I was given to understand that I might find her here.'

'You would have,' Christine replied, 'a week or so ago, but at the moment, she's on an assignment in Manchester.' The enigmatic stranger seemed disappointed. 'Look, I can give you a contact number,' she offered and virtually whispered, 'I know she'd be delighted to hear from you. I shouldn't say any more, but...' After writing down Melanie's details, she looked up. 'Tell me, just as a matter of interest, how did you manage to find us?'

'I've tried for a long time,' he admitted, 'but then saw you both on an early morning TV show.' He smiled briefly. 'After that, it was easy.'

Christine carefully folded the piece of paper and held it against her chest. 'Before I give you this, will you tell me how, being the author of *Straw Hat* and having been dead for fifteen years, you are here talking to me?'

The visitor sighed. 'I don't know how this misunderstanding has arisen, because I'm not and never have been a writer. All I ever did was come up with various ideas that I passed on to my older brother, John, who used them as the grounds for various novels.' A shadow passed across his handsome features as he glanced momentarily at the floor. 'Sadly, you see, it was my brother who passed away. You were discussing the power of ley lines and he seemed to deteriorate after visiting a place called Ley Farm. As you rightly said, it's a junction for these wretched trackways. Anyway,' he continued, 'my brother gradually became more and more confused before finally passing away. And, strangely, even the post-mortem could find no real cause for his death.' He paused. 'There's something about those lines that we don't fully understand and, you know, before that visit he was such a strong, healthy man with a mind like a razor.'

'I know. James Chronestead told us,' replied Christine, gently. 'And I'm so sorry.'

During this exchange, Karl had retreated to a seat at the back of the room and poured himself a drink. As Christine passed over her friend's details, she asked, 'May I know why you want to contact Melanie?'

Again, the tall visitor didn't respond immediately, as if uncertain quite how to reply. Finally, looking straight at Christine, he admitted, 'The fact is, when I first saw your friend, I knew I'd found someone very special.' He shrugged. 'But I'm shy and not very good with words. Anyway, I gathered up enough courage to approach her. It helped when I saw she was reading a copy of my brother's book, so I simply asked her whether she was enjoying it. Well, something like that.'

'Look,' interrupted Christine, 'we're being very inhospitable. Why don't you at least let me get you a drink?'

In response to such a warm invitation, the stranger from Menorca finally sat down. Then, with a glass in hand, he continued, 'But I think your friend suspected it was a come-on. Which, I suppose, it was in a way,' he admitted, with a slight smile. 'But you've got to start somewhere, haven't you? She certainly looked at me a bit suspiciously.' He toyed with his glass and said slowly, 'I think this is where the whole misunderstanding probably began, because, to stop her getting the wrong impression, I tried to explain that the story was my idea. But in any case, she didn't seem the slightest bit interested, so I just moved away. And that was it really.'

'Look,' she said quietly, 'there's something I need to tell you. But before I do, let me introduce myself. I'm Melanie's close friend, Christine, and I'm wondering perhaps if you could tell me your name.'

'That's no problem,' he smiled. 'I'm Peter. Peter Harris. But please, just call me Peter.'

'Well, Peter,' she began. 'I hope I'm not talking out of turn when I tell you that Melanie's often spoken about that time on the beach. Perhaps I shouldn't be saying this, but she was devastated when she thought you were dead. But you're not dead!' she enthused, thrusting the folded piece of paper into his hand. 'Now, don't waste a moment. Get in touch with her straightaway. But please, please try and break it gently when you tell her who you really are!'

Chapter 8

MELANIE FOUND THE city of Manchester a huge and impersonal place with loneliness becoming an ever-increasing problem. She felt lost in the sea of red brick buildings, many of which were a legacy of the Victorian era and in the process of demolition prior to development. In addition to all the brickery, people scurried about like ants – rushing, she suspected, they knew not where. It was the sort of world she hated – an endless festering warren of drab streets. She was just thankful for the luxury of her Mercedes, which insulated her from all the rat-race horror outside. Never, she thought gratefully, would she have to jostle her way along those dreary pavements. Her mind repeatedly returned to the one man who had so captured her imagination: a brief moment of magic on a faraway shore.

It was the first occasion Melanie had worked apart from Christine and she was missing her desperately. Boredom was difficult, for the assignment with Silk averaged barely two hours a day. The constant close-up clicking of cameras was an irritation designed to test the best of anyone's patience. Initially she'd thought of commuting from The Darchester, but had rejected the idea in favour of a suite of rooms in a local hotel. Now, however, she began to wonder if it had been the right decision, because after 3pm there was precious little to do except talk to the walls until bedtime. Television had never held much interest for her and the assortment of men she encountered, with their persistent overtures, always left her stone cold. Drearily kicking her red high-heeled shoes into the corner after one particularly tedious assignment, Melanie threw her designer handbag at the sofa and made for the drinks' cabinet. Finally, thoroughly fed-up, she decided to spend the evening at the cinema.

That night, Melanie barely managed an hour's sleep and awoke feeling tired and jaded. Without the reassurance of Christine's company, uncertainties about the future again began to close in. As her friend had pointed out, undoubtedly their champagne lifestyle couldn't last forever as age eroded the beauty nature had so kindly bestowed. She glanced down at her long shapely legs with their silky-smooth skin. Her legs had been ogled at by a thousand male eyes and probably fantasised over by a thousand others. But she knew only too well how disfigured it was possible for them to become. She had seen how her mother's legs had deteriorated over the years with varicose veins and a spider network of discolouration. It made Melanie shudder even to think about it. Although she dearly loved her adopted mother, she was just grateful they were not genetically related.

Getting off the bed, she crossed the room to gaze closely into the long wardrobe mirror. Only in her early twenties, she was happy to see a beautiful young woman gazing back at her. She leant forwards anxiously to examine the surface of her facial skin and the high cheekbones that were the hallmark of her allure. The same allure that had finally led to the downfall of her grandmother, Gerda Reinhardt, and she wondered briefly what had eventually become of her. Somehow, she felt close to Gerda, yet at the same time knew virtually nothing about her as a person: her hopes, her dreams and what sacrifices she must have made to risk being a spy. Was there a man she'd left back in Germany that she'd really loved? Had she planned to return one day and start a family with him? Or had she been in a similar situation to herself – in love with a frontline German soldier who had been killed fighting on the Russian front and was, therefore, forever beyond her reach. Melanie would never know and certainly had no means of ever finding out.

As she continued to study her features, heavy tresses of blonde hair kept getting in the way. She irritably brushed them aside in her search for the slightest blemish; imprints that would indicate the passage of time. Finally, though, she straightened up with a sigh of relief, satisfied there appeared no sign of deterioration.

The lack of sleep had left her feeling a dishevelled mess. She had little inclination to face another barrage of clicking cameras and the close proximity of their operators – some of whose personal hygiene was, at best, questionable. It was around 7am and as she sat on the stool of her dressing table after a quick shower, she pondered her options for the day. Brushing her hair into a high sheen, she was determined to escape the stifling confines of her job – if for only a few hours. Checking out of the hotel around 8am, she persuaded the receptionist to inform the Silk company of her temporary indisposition. Then, free at last and with keys in hand, she strode towards the car park and her Mercedes.

Stepping into the big white vehicle, Melanie luxuriated back into the deep leather upholstery. As a top model, she was paid huge dividends and this opened doors to worlds her parents could only have dreamt about. Finally, turning the ignition key, the powerful engine purred quietly into life, and easing the clutch, she spun the steering wheel before turning onto the Liverpool Road. Driving past the imposing landmark of Beetham Tower, she moved into Oxford Road that led out of the city.

After travelling south for a short distance, Melanie reached a wooded area. It was a popular beauty spot with tourists and being situated on high ground afforded extensive views over the sprawling metropolis. Turning into a small car park, she pulled up to relax and just gaze out at the panoramic view. It was from such a distance that the growing dominance of high-rise apartments became all too apparent. Victorian Manchester, like London, was slowly succumbing to a sea of glass and concrete.

However, Melanie wasn't just there to get a perspective of Manchester, but rather one of her own destiny. Unaware of the developments back in London, she again brooded on the only man who had ever meant anything to her. Sadly, she still believed him to be forever beyond the one gap in life that can never be bridged. Her eyes took in the towering spire of St Mary's Church, a symbol of so much faith. Other huge places of worship stood awaiting demolition; the work of hands belonging to a devotional generation long gone. Again, she wondered over the sheer unbelievable cruelty of death.

Melanie's mind turned to the words of the aging editor, James Chronestead, and his theory concerning ley lines. Was it really conceivable that the author of *Straw Hat* had somehow cheated death and gained an extra day through their power? At first, she'd dismissed the idea as nonsense. Now, however, sitting in her car and gazing out at the sea of buildings as they basked in the greyness of an early November day, she began to seriously consider what the future might hold. She had no siblings that she knew of, so there seemed little alternative to an eventual lonely old age – something she had always dreaded.

Again, she could see the tall handsome stranger emerging from the Mediterranean... but it had all been so brief. Oh, so brief. Suddenly coming to a decision, she reached across to the glove compartment and removed a writing pad. For several moments, she sat with her pen poised, but then began to write.

Chapter 9

WHEN PETER HAD so unexpectedly turned up at Christine's hotel and declared his feelings for Melanie, her first thoughts had been to warn her friend. The initial shock of opening the door and finding him standing there had been terrifying, and she was anxious to protect her companion from a similar experience. However, although she tried to contact her several times that evening, it was to no avail. Her first attempt had only drawn the standard, 'Sorry, there is a fault. Please try again later.' Subsequent efforts were equally ineffectual. So, early the following morning, she phoned the hotel itself, only to experience similar frustration as a rather condescending female voice informed her that Melanie had checked out about 8am. Wondering where Melanie could have gone and why, she terminated the call and returned the mobile to her handbag. However, no sooner had she snapped it shut than the phone started screaming for attention.

'Hello. Who's calling?' she asked.

'Sorry to trouble you,' came a low male voice, which she instantly recognised as Peter. 'I must apologise for giving you such a fright the other day. I really am very sorry. But, as I explained, I had no idea there was a misunderstanding of the situation or I would have at least phoned first or written.'

He was obviously genuinely sincere, and Christine was quick to respond. 'Oh, that's fine, Peter. It really is. Don't give it another thought.'

Her caller continued. 'I've tried the number you gave me for Melanie several times, but there seems to be some kind of problem. I don't suppose you've got an address for her by any chance?'

'I have,' replied Christine, cautiously. 'Although it's a question of catching her in, because I tried phoning her this morning and was told she left about 8am. I also tried an email but haven't had a response, so all I can do is wait for her to contact me.'

However, when that contact finally occurred, it left Christine in a state of high anxiety.

After the delay caused by Peter's phone call, Christine knew she would be hard pressed to meet her assignment at the ITV studios anywhere near on time. Any little hope she had left was finally dashed when she arrived at the hotel reception and one of the assistants called her over.

'Excuse me, Miss Elliott, but this letter arrived for you this morning.'

Christine was in a hurry and any delay was irksome, until she recognised the handwriting belonging to her friend. Frantically short of time, she made the fatal error of stuffing it in her handbag with the full intention of reading it at the first opportunity. Unfortunately, her desperately late arrival at the studio had brought the producer of the early morning show to a state of near neurotic collapse.

'Where the hell have you been!?' he just about spluttered. 'Don't you realise you're on any moment now.'

Christine knew, and knew only too well, as she dashed for her dressing room to find the latest designer fashions awaiting her attention. The whole situation was not helped by the anxious clucking noises made by the presenter as he frantically fidgeted to and fro outside. He was obviously on the verge of wetting himself.

Sensing his explosive state, she called out irritably, 'Alright. Alright. I'm coming, but if you must have an orgasm, for goodness' sake go and do it somewhere else and not outside my dressing room.'

Finally, he ushered her on to the brightly lit studio floor amidst a barrage of cameras. To the casual observer, everything appeared perfectly smooth and professionally presented. No one knew about the ferment that had gone on behind the scenes and the model's pressing need to read her friend's letter. But then, as if to heighten her anxiety, Christine suddenly realised she had a second appearance at 10am on ITV2. So, it was well after 11.30am by the time she'd returned to her dressing room and finally tore open the letter, only to be mortified by what she read.

My dearest Christine,

I have recently been giving my position a great deal of serious thought. We've been together for a number of years, but now you have Karl and a new life is opening up for you in which I will have no part. And while I am very happy for you, I have a real fear of ending up alone.

I hope you will understand when I say there has only ever been one man in my life that has meant anything and, after our discussion with James Chronestead, I have decided to take a week from work and risk crossing the lines at Ley Farm. I feel it might be my only chance of us ever being together. So, wish me well.

Lastly, may I thank you for your loving friendship.
Goodbye, my dear friend.
Melanie
xxx

'She's mad! She's absolutely mad,' muttered the auburn-haired model while reaching for her mobile phone. Then, checking the time, she desperately dialled Peter's number and waited impatiently while it rang. It was now vital they intercepted Melanie before it was too late. To her absolute frustration, though, all she received was a metallic-sounding female voice informing her there was no one to answer her call but to leave a message.

'Peter!' she began urgently, 'Melanie is on her way to the ley line intersection at Ley Farm. Please, please call me back immediately when you get this message, because I believe she intends to cross it in some lunatic attempt to find you.'

The failure to contact Peter only served to heighten the urgency of everything. Christine found herself pacing frantically up and down the ITV2 corridors. She did not have long to wait, however, before her mobile trilled into life. Snatching it from her bag, she replied with a desperate, 'Hello!'

'It's me, Peter,' came his reassuring voice. 'I thought Melanie was supposed to be in Manchester for the next few weeks. But look,' he added, 'never mind that. Just tell me where you are, and I'll come and join you at once.'

By this stage in her career, Christine had splashed out on a new Ferrari, and she sat waiting anxiously in the studio car park for his arrival. Finally, the passenger door swung open and he jumped in.

'Am I glad to see you,' she sighed in relief.

'Whatever we do,' he urged, 'we must stop Melanie crossing those ley lines. I honestly believe they killed my brother.' Then, turning in his seat, he asked, 'I suppose you're absolutely sure it's today she's going to try?'

Christine nodded. 'Well, I can't be absolutely certain, but the postmark is yesterday's date and it's the only clue we've got.' Then, passing over Melanie's letter, she added, 'Here. See for yourself.'

After quickly scanning the note, he looked up doubtfully. 'Hmm. The trouble is,' he observed, 'she doesn't specify any actual time. For all we know, we could already be facing a *fait accompli*.'

'Well, it's approaching 12.30pm now,' mused Christine. 'And if I know Melanie, she'd never be out of bed much before 9am. Well, not unless she absolutely had to. But, I mean, how long do you think it would take her to get from Manchester down to rural Mid Sussex? It's a long way.'

Peter leant back with a sigh. 'Possibly we might be in with a chance. Let's see. If she comes down the M6, which ultimately leads to London, and then joins the M25 and on to the M23, it will take about four hours.' He again looked doubtful. 'Even if we leave now, it'll be touch-and-go. Then, of course, a lot depends on the type of car she's driving.'

'It's a fast car,' replied Christine. 'It's a Mercedes.'

'Well, it won't take her long in something like that,' he retorted. 'So, let's get moving. I'll show you the way as we go.'

'Oh, don't worry!' she replied. 'I've got the satnav.'

'Forget it,' he retorted. 'I don't trust them. They lead you all over the wherever except the one place you want to go. Trust me, I know where Ley Farm is.'

'Okay, but keep a look out for the police, Peter,' she whispered, as they moved out of London onto the northern end of the southbound M23. 'Because I'm going to put my foot down.'

The Ferrari was a thoroughbred, and, within seconds, they were doing well over 120mph.

'Nice car,' he admired.

'Nice money,' she smiled, glancing at his profile – a profile capable of turning the head of any woman. She could well understand her friend's fascination with him.

They raced south for some thirty minutes, hoping to catch a glimpse of Melanie's white car. Then, about some twenty miles north of Brighton, Peter suddenly instructed Christine to branch west at the Bolney junction. This road gradually petered out into a series of winding narrow lanes that caused Christine to drastically reduce speed.

Peter leant forwards as the landscape became ever more familiar. 'We're getting pretty close,' he warned. The meandering terrain, however, had become ever more difficult to negotiate, with hairpin bends obscuring any oncoming traffic and causing Christine to reduce speed still further. The problem was also aggravated by the undulating nature of the area. Nevertheless, as they topped one particular hill, Peter suddenly called out excitedly, 'I think I can see her car. It's about a mile ahead.' As they drove on down into the next dip, he lost sight of it and, fearful they would be too late, he urged Christine to go a little faster.

'I can't,' she protested. 'It's dangerous enough as it is on these vicious bends. I hate driving in such conditions – especially,' she emphasised, *under pressure.*'

'Look,' he offered. 'Would you like me to drive?'

However, nobody was going to sit behind the wheel of her precious Ferrari, although the offer suddenly became academic as, rounding the next curve, they found themselves confronted by the business end of a line of slow-moving horses. Several of them were thoughtlessly being ridden two-abreast.

'Oh no,' growled Peter. 'That's put an end to any chance we might have had.'

Chapter 10

COMPLETELY FRUSTRATED, PETER reached across and sounded the horn several times despite the fact that he knew such actions ran strictly contrary to the Highway Code. You just don't make sudden noises near horses. However, he was beyond caring, judiciously signalling for them to get the hell out of the way. It was rude behaviour and the lead rider responded by unmentionable use of his riding crop. Nevertheless, the small group wasted no time in retreating into the first available lay-by.

Peter feared the delay had been costly, for as they crested the next high piece of ground, the entrance to Ley Farm was just about visible in the distance. Being early November and approaching 2pm, it was classically grey and overcast, which, together with the development of a fine drizzle, did little to help.

'Can you see her?' asked Christine, anxiously.

Peter shook his head. 'I just hope and pray she's changed her mind. By the way,' he exclaimed, 'I don't know if old Chronestead told you, but it's the smaller of the two gates we've got to watch for. Nobody ever uses it because they know only too well that's where the danger lies. Well, nobody, that is, except my poor

153

brother,' he added bitterly. 'But that was years ago and it's probably overgrown by now. So, she won't find it easy.'

They were now rounding the final bend before the stretch that led straight to the farm and were just in time to see Melanie approaching the gate on foot. Peter immediately wound down his side window.

'Melanie, don't! Don't do it!'

However, they were still some way off and, with the wind in his face, it was impossible to make himself heard. It seemed as if the hand of fate was against them, because as they emerged from the final bend, it was to find a fallen tree blocking the narrow lane and Melanie's white Mercedes lying abandoned in a nearby ditch.

'Wait there!' ordered Peter, jumping from the car. 'I'll try and stop her,' he called back as he raced towards the farm.

'Melanie! Melanie!' he repeatedly shouted. But against the heightening wind, it was useless. He could only watch as she reached the densely overgrown entrance. It was further than he'd realised. Even running as hard as he could, he knew he'd never reach her in time. He hoped she might glance round, but her attention was fully focused on the gate. To his horror, she started to try and force her way through. But the briars that had ensnared the woodwork were reluctant to release their vice-like grip. So, with renewed hope, Peter redoubled his efforts. However, Melanie had both hands on top of the gate and was wrenching at it with all her strength.

Chapter 11

EARLIER THAT DAY, a very different drama had been unfolding on the approach to Heathrow Airport. Karl von Jörgensen was piloting an early overnight World Airways flight from New York. The sky was streaked with light on the eastern horizon and they were still some four hundred miles off the west coast of Ireland. One of the air hostesses tapped on the door of the cockpit. Turning from the bright rows of his control panel, Karl released the security catch and found himself faced with a very anxious young lady. 'What is it, Kate?' he asked.

'Well, sir,' she replied. 'There seems to be a small stream of smoke coming from behind the left engine. It's not there all the time and I don't think any of the passengers have noticed it – well, not yet, anyway.' She hesitated. 'It's just that I thought you should know, sir.'

Karl had taken the girl in at a glance. She was pretty and fresh-faced, and her uniform was a credit to the airline, while her enthusiasm had been obvious from the day she joined the company. She was, in fact, a shining example of her generation.

'Thank you, Kate,' he nodded. 'I'll attend to it immediately – oh, and by the way, there's no need to alarm the passengers.' And with that, the flight attendant withdrew while Karl turned to his co-pilot. 'I can't see any indication of overheating on the monitors,' he observed, glancing at the bank of controls.

'Hang on a minute, though,' rejoined his fellow pilot. 'I thought the left-side monitor flickered for a moment just then.' Both men watched carefully, but they could detect no further movement of the needle.

'I think, as a precaution,' suggested Karl, 'that we should contact Shannon Airport and request the possibility of an emergency landing. Incidentally, how far are we from the coast?'

After checking the relevant data, his co-pilot estimated there were about three hundred and sixty miles to go. 'And that,' he added, 'is supposing they even have the capacity to handle an airliner of this size.' However, Karl decided to go ahead and send out a mayday call.

'Hello, Shannon. This is flight 109 of World Airways, carrying three hundred and thirty-five passengers on course from New York to Heathrow, with an approximate arrival time of 0630. We're still about some three hundred odd miles off the Irish coast, but may have developed engine trouble and might need assistance.'

The response was prompt and reassuring. 'Hello, flight 109. This is Shannon Airport. We estimate you could be with us in the next two hours. And should

156

you need our assistance, the western airstrip will be made available. Also, in the event of an emergency landing, we will have all relevant agencies and facilities standing by on full alert. Good luck and out.'

The aircraft cruised on for approximately half an hour without further incident and it began to look as though they would reach Heathrow on schedule, but then the co-pilot observed anxiously, 'That left engine sounds to be running a bit rough to me.'

The words were scarcely out of his mouth when there came another urgent knocking on the cabin door. This time, it was one of the older flight attendants. She looked pale and frightened. 'It's the left engine, sir. There are small flames coming from the top of the cowling.'

Karl had worked with Esther for a long time. He knew her to be a reliable and calm member of the crew. 'It's alright, Esther. There's no need to panic. It can easily be extinguished,' he assured her, while operating the appropriate control. 'Can you go back and tell me how the thing looks now?'

'I don't know how things look now,' interrupted an anxious co-pilot, 'but I can tell you that engine's running very badly. And I wouldn't be surprised if we lose power that side altogether.'

Karl checked the milometer. 'It's about one hour's flying time before we reach the Irish coast.' Then, under his breath, he added, 'I just hope we make it.'

'Well, we're going to have to make it – on the right engine,' observed his fellow officer. 'Because I've just shut off the left as a precaution.'

Even as he spoke, Esther reappeared at the entrance. 'There're only a few puffs of steam coming from the top of the engine now, sir,' she reported – but then asked with a touch of fear, 'We will make it, won't we, sir?'

The captain smiled and nodded. 'Of course, we will.' He then turned to the intercom and sounded the familiar jingle. 'This is the captain speaking. You may be aware of the overheating problems we are experiencing with the left engine. There is no cause for alarm, but we may have to make an emergency landing at Shannon Airport. In the meantime, please make sure your seatbelts are securely fastened.'

All this was happening long before Christine was awake and received the apologetic call from Peter, so she had no idea of the possible danger her man might be facing.

Chapter 12

MEANWHILE, STRUGGLING ON one engine, the crippled airliner agonisingly crawled its way towards the distant beaches of Ireland. Gradually, the time gap narrowed to an hour, then to three-quarters. However, when barely thirty minutes from the coast, the recalcitrant engine suddenly erupted into a mass of flames that began to lick along the side of the main fuselage. As the screams of the passengers rang in his ears, Karl fleetingly wondered if he'd ever see his beloved Christine again.

He turned to his ashen-faced co-pilot. 'If we don't do something, either that wing's going to fall off or the whole plane will go up in a ball of fire.'

'So, what do you suggest then?' exclaimed his horrified co-pilot. 'That we try and ditch in the sea?'

Karl shook his head. 'No. My grandfather flew Junkers 88s and Heinkels. They were German bombers. On one occasion, he put the Junkers into a steep dive to extinguish fire caused by incendiary bullets. And that,' he exclaimed emphatically, 'is just what I intend to do.'

'But this is a huge commercial airliner,' protested his companion. 'You can't just throw it about the sky as if it were some fighter plane. Besides, it's against all the regulations.' However, Karl had made up his mind and was not the type to be deterred by deskbound regulators.

Pandemonium had broken out among the passengers. Some were crying out in terror while others prayed for God to spare them. The stewardesses were excellent, and they did their best to keep things calm. It was an impossible task. After all, how do you placate people who are convinced their lives are about to be horrifyingly terminated? One young man, demented with terror, was down on his knees, beating the aisle floor with his fists. 'I don't want to die! I don't want to die!' he screamed. The stewardess tried to persuade him back to his seat.

The plane's jingle sounded once again.

'Attention. This is the captain. I regret to inform you that we are faced with an emergency. It is essential that all passengers remain seated and calm. In the unlikely event that we have to touchdown on the water, ensure you carry out the correct procedures of escape as demonstrated by the cabin crew. In the meantime, please adopt the brace position as we drop some ten thousand feet. I will warn you when this is about to occur.'

Whatever one's opinion might be of air hostesses, they rose to the occasion magnificently. Rushing up and down the aisle, they seemed to be everywhere at once trying to reassure the passengers. One young mother was hysterically clutching her baby and screaming, 'No! No!' at the top of her voice. Esther, who had been attending a sickly older man, immediately rushed to her side.

'Look,' she said gently, putting her arm around the woman. 'I've known Captain Jörgensen for many years and he's the most confident pilot I've ever met. If anyone can save us, he's the man that can do it.' *And good-looking,* she thought, wistfully, sensing that he was probably already spoken for.

However, a quite different scenario was unfolding in the cockpit where the atmosphere was tense and far from cordial.

'With all due respect, sir,' the co-pilot almost shouted. 'If we do what you suggest, it could tear the left wing off altogether and send us spiralling completely out of control. We could hit the water with such force, the whole thing would totally disintegrate.' Then, without even pausing for breath, he added, 'At least drop down slowly so that we could try to float the thing and give the passengers a chance to use the escape procedure with their lifejackets.'

'Sorry,' retorted Karl, 'but we're doing it my way.' The side of his nature that had seen him flattening the hotel assistant was hovering dangerously below the surface. Thoroughly irritated, he added, 'Now, keep your place and tell me what altitude we're at.'

'Forty-one thousand feet, sir,' replied his co-pilot, while straining to maintain some semblance of professionalism. 'But, sir,' he persisted, 'even if the wing stays in place, there won't be enough power to level off with just one engine before we hit the water.'

His pleadings were all to no avail. Karl again spoke through the intercom. 'Take the brace position everybody. We're going down.'

Unfortunately, just before he sent the giant aircraft into a headlong plunge, Karl made the fatal mistake of loosening his harness to take a final look back along the affected fuselage. The plane assumed a ninety-degree angle to the earth as gravity took over. Its speed became breathtaking, dropping at thousands of feet per second. The rush of air was unbelievable. Just as he had predicted, the fire was almost immediately snuffed out.

Karl turned to his co-pilot. 'What did I tell you? They called the technique "feathering" during the Battle of Britain air war.'

'But this is not World War II and we're down to twenty-eight thousand feet,' he shouted back. 'You'll never level off in time.'

However, slowly but surely, Karl managed to coax the nose of the great airliner up from its headlong descent. 'Come on, come on,' he gritted, straining at the controls.

'Twenty-five thousand feet,' parroted the co-pilot. 'Twenty-two thousand, twenty thousand.'

But by this time, Karl had miraculously managed to bring the giant airliner back onto an even keel. Turning to his sweating assistant, he ordered him to check the state of the ruined wing.

'Well, it's still there,' he reported, after getting up and glancing along the body of the plane. 'But it's in a very shaky state. I just hope it holds until we reach

Shannon.' Although relieved, he sounded resentful after the way Karl had spoken. It didn't help knowing he was German either. He'd once heard there was no such thing as a national stereotype, but the pilot's arrogant behaviour made him wonder.

'I'm minimising the speed to nurse the wing,' explained the captain. 'I estimate we're now about twenty minutes or less from Ireland.' Painfully and nail-bitingly slowly, the minutes ticked away. Fifteen. Ten. All the time, the co-pilot monitored the damaged wing. Finally, Karl spotted the distant coast, which was now clearly visible. It had been early dawn when the drama first started, but now it had become broad daylight. 'We're going to make it,' Karl muttered. 'We're going to make it.'

The aircraft was down to less than fifteen-thousand feet, as Karl flicked on the radio. 'Hello, Shannon. Hello, Shannon. This is flight 109 on mayday alert and again requesting permission to land. We should be with you in approximately fifteen minutes.'

'Hello, mayday flight 109,' came back the immediate response. 'Permission granted. The most western runway is now clear for your approach. Good luck and out.'

Chapter 13

PASSING OVER THE Atlantic border of Southern Ireland, Karl detected a faint cheering from the passengers, whereas earlier there'd only been the sounds of terror.

'I don't know what they're so happy about,' muttered the second-in-command. 'We're now down to less than fifteen-thousand feet and getting lower all the time.'

'They're alive,' snapped Karl. 'They're alive and grateful for it.'

His fellow pilot was quiet for a while before observing, 'We're still losing height. At the moment, we're around thirteen thousand five hundred,' and he again looked back to check the shattered wing.

Gradually, they limped towards their goal. At that height, and with little local cloud, the outlines of fields and roads were clearly visible, while to their right the Shannon Estuary shimmered in the early morning light. But even as Karl looked down, there came a rending noise from the direction of the left side.

'The wing tip's gone!' he exclaimed, in response to his companion's worried look. 'It won't help, but we'll manage.'

Then, something occurred that sent even the resolute and cool-headed Karl into a spin. Suddenly, the right engine faltered, picked up, then finally cut out altogether. This left them completely powerless and with no alternative but to just glide: a failure that was likely to cost both speed and height – neither of which they could afford to lose.

'There's no immediate danger,' observed Karl, 'but we might have to ditch in one of the fields. Goodness only knows, there're enough of them. The real danger, of course, is stalling. What's our present height?'

'Down to under eleven thousand feet, sir,' came the terse reply.

'And our air speed?'

The ongoing emergency had taken its toll on Karl and the strain was clearly beginning to show on his face. 'Bloody nuisance,' he breathed. 'And we're only about ten minutes from Shannon. You'd think the effing plane was jinxed.'

'Sir, if you'll excuse me. You've not secured your safety harness tight enough.'

Karl, however, was too otherwise engaged as he attempted to refire the right engine and his co-pilot's warning never registered.

'I just hope the fuel supply that side hasn't been affected,' he muttered at his third attempt. This latest effort did the trick and the jet finally roared back into life. 'Thank God! We're almost there,' he breathed, leaning forwards in his seat. 'Hello, Shannon. This is flight 109. We are now approaching your western runway.'

The relief in both the cockpit and the body of the plane was tangible as the huge airliner approached the airstrip. But it was a premature relief, for, as they prepared to touchdown, a horrendous noise of tortured metal could be heard throughout the aircraft. Sickeningly, the whole crippled left engine and its damaged wing finally tore away from the main body of the plane. This was absolutely disastrous. The aircraft was completely unbalanced. Now, with lift only coming from the right side, the plane keeled over and dropped like a stone. Karl had reduced speed to a minimum, but the impact with the ground was enormous. Amidst the sound of smashing glass and the screeching of tormented metal, together with the screaming of the passengers, the damaged plane carved a long deep groove in the tarmac. Finally, it shuddered to a standstill on its side. Dense clouds of dust arose, which obscured the whole horrific scene. The co-pilot would remember the sounds of the terrified passengers until his dying day and vowed never to fly again.

Viewed from a safe distance, it was a spectacular drama, but was far from spectacular for those on board. However, the authorities at Shannon had been very thorough and it seemed that almost immediately the wreckage was surrounded by fire trucks and ambulances, while medics and first aid people swarmed everywhere.

While all this was taking place, a blissfully ignorant Christine was just waking up. As she stretched luxuriously, she remembered to expect a call from Karl to confirm his arrival at Heathrow around midday. Little could she have known what actually awaited her.

After such a serious crash, the rescue teams were expecting to find, if not death, at least many seriously injured people. But, amazingly, although the passengers had been badly shaken up, apart from one woman who had sustained a broken leg, miraculously there appeared to be little more than minor cuts and bruises. As one of the medics observed, 'You were lucky to have such a brilliant pilot to get you out of an impossible situation. He must be a man in a million!'

'Here, here,' agreed several of the passengers, partly in response to the sheer relief of still being alive.

However, that was not enough for one public-spirited woman, who, although in the same traumatised state as everyone else and with a nasty gash along her forehead, nevertheless lavished even more praise on the pilot. 'Yes,' she called out. 'Weren't we lucky to have such a wonderful captain? And I believe we're only alive today thanks to his courage and skill. So, I call for three cheers for our brave pilot.'

Even the emergency teams joined in, but as the chorus of approval echoed around the wreckage, they failed to register in the very ears for which they were intended. Those ears would never hear anything again. Captain Karl von Jörgensen was dead; slumped over the very controls he'd struggled with for so long. Sadly, in his concern for the plane and the welfare of his passengers, he'd neglected to heed his co-pilot's warning to tighten his safety harness. Tragically, when the plane had finally hit the tarmac, there had been nothing to prevent him being hurled against his instrument panel with such force that he died almost instantly from head injuries. Ironically, he was the only fatality on board and, as the news of his death spread among the passengers, the sadness was palpable.

By the time Karl's body had finally and reverently been lifted from its resting place, Christine had read Melanie's letter and was on her way with Peter in an attempt to stop her making the biggest mistake of her life.

Chapter 14

DESPITE OUTSIDE EFFORTS, Melanie had finally managed to reach her goal and was striving to open the gate. She paused for a moment, thinking someone had called her name. Listening carefully, she decided it was a trick of the wind. It wasn't, of course. It was Peter frantically trying to get her attention. Sadly, and without looking back, she renewed the onslaught on her objective – even though, by now, any actual trace of the ancient trackways had long since succumbed to the debris of time.

The fear of approaching change had resulted in a devastating impact on Melanie. One thing was certain, the constant trekking to various fashion venues on her own was out of the question. The prospect of a career in the cut-throat atmosphere of Hollywood amounted to a nightmare beyond imagination. Instead, her chief concern now was to find the one man she had found so captivating – who, by the irony of fate, was only mere yards behind her.

The earlier fine rain had gradually become a downpour and was soaking both herself and the gate. To make matters worse, the wind had increased its ferocity and was roaring through the numerous trees that bent and swayed under the onslaught. Meanwhile, Peter and Christine had reached the final straight and, although he shouted at the top of his voice, he might just as well have opened his mouth and remained silent.

There was barely a matter of a hundred yards between them, but Peter could only watch helplessly as Melanie finally forced her way into the farm. Utterly frustrated, he came to a breathless halt where all he could do was witness events as they unfolded.

Sometimes people set out on a mission with little or no concept of how it can be achieved. This was the case with Melanie, for, as she stepped beyond the gate, she had absolutely no idea of what to expect or even what to do next. Straight ahead, in the pouring rain, was the setting depicted in the book *Straw Hat*, with its long-unmade drive that drained surplus water into a huge fishing lake on the right.

The utter lack of life was chilling. Though the location was set in the depths of rural Sussex, and, essentially, farming country, there was no sign of any animals. No sheep, no cattle, not even the odd chicken. The great fish lake looked dead and completely incapable of supporting anything. Melanie's only companions in the grey conditions were the howling wind and blinding rain, which made her feel lonely and afraid – everything, in fact, she'd always dreaded. Was this really, she wondered, the location once adopted by the author she'd gone to such lengths to find?

Immediately in front of her lay the huge farmhouse kitchen window that looked out over the lake. A place where the fictitious John had stood and gazed from on many occasions. In the story, bright light would have streamed out in welcome, whereas now it only appeared bleak and forbidding.

Melanie hesitated as the great oak farmhouse front door swung slowly back as if by its own volition, for there was no one to be seen. It was almost as though some unknown entity was inviting her to enter the dark and mysterious depths of the house. She shivered at the thought of what might lie in wait there. A streak of horror ran through Melanie as she felt a slight irritation in her scalp and saw a section of her blonde hair slowly drifting towards the ground. Worse was to come, because in going to retrieve the lock, she found it all but impossible to bend down. Inexplicably stiff, there was no flexibility in her back.

Terrified by what was happening, the model also noticed how weak she was beginning to feel as ever more of her hair fell from her head. Looking down at the backs of her normally smooth hands, she gasped at their hideous appearance. They were now gnarled and ridden with veins while her manicured nails had become vicious claw-like talons. Frantically, she clutched at her face, but its velvet-like quality had become replaced by a repulsive wrinkled gauntness. Her adventure through the ley line intersection had come at a fearful price, for it had accelerated the nightmare of all women – that of growing old.

As the advancing decay continued, it became increasingly difficult to remain upright and she was being forced into a stoop-like posture. Glancing about from her bent position, she was just in time to see the remains of her once beautiful hair being scattered away across the lake. Too late, she realised that she had become an old woman in a matter of moments, but the progressive process was far from over and, as what little remaining strength finally slipped away, she felt herself falling to the ground – effectively dying.

All this had taken place very quickly and the instant Peter saw Melanie fall down, he took the main five-bar gate in a single bound. As he reached her side, however, he immediately recoiled in revulsion at what met his gaze. Now lying on her back, with barely the strength to raise her head, was an unrecognisable old crone. Obviously close to death, Melanie's clothes hung loosely on her wasted body, while with sunken eyes and cheeks she presented a truly fearful sight.

Crouching down beside the stricken woman, he could hardly believe his eyes.

'Melanie,' he began, but then words failed him because, at her rate of degeneration, it was obvious that the vivacious woman he'd so long dreamt about would soon be little more than a heap of ash. For a brief moment, he thought he saw her cracked lips move and he bent down to try and hear what she was struggling to say.

'You came,' he just about heard her whisper. She then barely managed to croak, 'Hold me.' And lowering his head still further, he was just in time to catch her final plea. 'Please.'

But still he hesitated at the revolting prospect of actually touching the disintegrating and shapeless heap that had once been a beautiful human being. Again, the lips quivered in a last supplication, but the effort proved too great and no actual sound emerged.

Overpowered by pathos and sorrow, Peter braced himself and closed his eyes. Then, reaching for the shrunken and sodden bundle, he slowly but tenderly lifted it from the ground and gently held her close. However, to a man of his size and strength, she weighed virtually nothing. Through his still closed eyelids, he felt the tears force their way through.

So, with her head resting in the crook of his arm, he turned back towards the entrance. Christine was standing there with her head bowed against the driving weather and with tears in her eyes.

'Is she...?' she asked. 'Is she...?'

But Peter was dumb with misery and merely shook his head. 'Too late,' he finally managed, brokenly. 'It's too late.' And squinting against the fierce rain, he leant over and gently kissed the shrivelled lips. But then, addressing Christine again, indicated the five-bar gate. 'If you'd be kind enough to open that for me, we'll get out of this hellhole and take her back to my place.'

He had to shout above the gale, but Christine was not the only one who heard him, because, miraculously, Melanie was beginning to wake up as if from some deep, dreamless sleep. At the same time, she started to feel the warmth of life flowing back into her decayed body. Once clear of the farm entrance, it did seem his burden felt slightly heavier, but he dismissed it as the ever-increasing pressure of the wind. Finally, the difference became undeniable – especially when the two hands that had been hanging down so lifelessly suddenly closed round the back of his neck.

Peter was unable to believe what was happening. He was overcome by a sudden flood of joy as he looked down to see the beautiful and lovely girl that had so haunted his heart.

'You're alive again!' Melanie exclaimed, her eyes shining as she snuggled closer into his shoulder. 'It was worth all the risk and nearly dying to find you.'

'Look,' he shouted, 'I've never been dead. It was all a mistake in the first place. But let's get out of this storm and into the car.' Once in the shelter of the back of the Ferrari, he gasped incredulously, 'You risked crossing the ley lines just to find me!'

'That's because I love you!' she exclaimed.

'But how can you love me? You hardly know me,' he protested, while gazing into her eyes. 'Well, apart from that brief encounter on the beach.'

'Let me put it this way,' she explained, excitedly, if a little brazenly, 'I fancied you something rotten from the moment I first saw you, and the more I've thought about it, the more I came to realise you're the only man for me.'

'But,' he protested, 'you didn't show the slightest interest originally.'

She hugged him tighter than ever. 'I know, I know,' she admitted bitterly. 'And I've regretted it ever since!'

For them, the pouring rain and driving wind that had been buffeting the car no longer seemed to exist as he gazed into her deep blue eyes.

Meanwhile, Christine was sitting patiently in front behind the steering wheel. 'Don't mind me,' she smiled. 'I won't look.'

'So, you see,' Melanie continued, 'you've been in my thoughts from that first meeting.' She shrugged. 'But I've had the misery of thinking you were dead.'

He shook his head. 'No. That was my brother. But, you know, I've thought about you so many times, wondering who you might be and whether you were in a relationship with someone. And you can't imagine the courage it took to find you.'

'Tell me?' she asked curiously. 'Why did you originally call yourself John Grant – the man portrayed in *Straw Hat*?'

He looked momentarily embarrassed.

'Oh, just put it down to a childish whim. I suppose I admired the character of my brother's creation and liked to identify with him. Silly, really,' he added ruefully. 'And very misleading.'

As he held her lightly, he suddenly realised the cause of her restoration. It wasn't the fact of bracing himself to pick up the wasted remains of a once beautiful showgirl. It was rather the combination of their feelings for each other – feelings that excluded anything and anyone else. A force so great as to overcome any obstacle. Even the occult power of the ley lines.

Love – the greatest power on earth – advocated by the greatest man who ever walked the earth – a man called Jesus Christ.

Christine was overjoyed by her friend's happiness, little knowing that her own had come to a violent and abrupt end several hours earlier.

Chapter 15

WHEN CHRISTINE FINALLY learned of Karl's death the following day, she was completely devastated and remained so to a greater or lesser extent for the rest of her life. She never got over the loss of the man who had so impetuously insisted she be his fiancée and have his treasured family ring – something she wore with pride and devotion until the day she died. She never married, preferring rather to remain single and loyal to his memory. Even her last will and testament insisted she be buried next to his final resting place – along with the ring she had so treasured. It's doubtful, though, whether the sticky-fingered undertakers, eventually responsible for her funeral, would have permitted such a valuable piece of jewellery to actually stay with her.

Karl's funeral was a desperately sad affair, but it was, nevertheless, a very dignified and touching occasion. Literally everyone who had been through the terrifying ordeal of Flight 109 was there for the ceremony. In fact, the hushed church was packed with World Airline staff, family members and sympathetic representatives of the public. Down one side of the aisle, every available off-duty pilot faced a similar line of flight attendants – all of whom were dressed in full official company uniform. Every man and woman in that sad avenue stood reverently with bowed heads as Karl's casket passed slowly by. He was borne by six of his colleagues – one of whom had been his co-pilot – as they solemnly made their way up the aisle to the altar at the east end.

High above, brilliant-coloured lights sparkled from the stained-glass windows and contrasted strangely with the grim proceedings below. They depicted saints with the prospect of a better life to come and, as she gazed about, Christine wondered whether there was any hope in their promise. She was sure of one thing, though: her faithful friend, Melanie, would remain by her side during the entire fateful day.

Sometimes, one thinks of such occasions as happening in damp and miserable conditions, but on the day of Karl's final journey, it was quite the reverse. Although early in December, the weather had been bright, if slightly chilly. However, as the last of the autumn sun in the cemetery gradually slipped down towards the western horizon, and after expressing their last condolences, people began to drift off from that field of sadness to go their various ways. With the continuing advance of evening, the shadows in that lonely place became ever longer and began to create an eerie crochet of patterns across the sea of gravestones. Eventually, even Karl's grieving parents realised it was time to go and bade Christine farewell.

'*Auf wiedersehen*. We are so sorry,' murmured Karl's elderly father. And, after a departing hug, they too slowly turned away. Their arms closely round each other for support, they made their way back through the maze of tombs to their waiting car. Now both late in life, Christine watched them go with a certain pang of envy and loss, for even after all those years together, they were still obviously very much in love.

Finally, she found herself standing alone at the foot of Karl's flower-covered resting place and reflected on the irony of life. It had always been Melanie who had feared being alone, whereas now, paradoxically, it was she who faced an isolated future. Despite all Karl's impetuousness and sometimes eccentric ways, there would never be anyone else to take his place. Even as she continued to stand there in the midst of sadness, she felt the arm of her friend slip round her shoulders and knew Melanie's friendship would never die.

If I should spend my whole life through
And yet miss that one transcending moment
Then, surely, I would have to ask
What was the purpose of my journey in the
first place?

Epilogue

It's ironic that Melanie had feared the spectre of loneliness thinking her man to be dead, while her friend, Christine, chose to live a life alone knowing her man was gone forever. Surely, it tempts one to wonder whether some thing or some force is toying with our human lives. I wonder, indeed.

This book is printed on paper from sustainable sources managed under the Forest Stewardship Council (FSC) scheme.

It has been printed in the UK to reduce transportation miles and their impact upon the environment.

For every new title that Matador publishes, we plant a tree to offset CO_2, partnering with the More Trees scheme.

For more about how Matador offsets its environmental impact, see www.troubador.co.uk/about/